Ellie Mann

ARINT SARATIR: WARRIOR'S LIGHT

Taylor J. Beisler

Eloquent Books
New York, New York

Wayxa Sea
Valley fields
Falls Landing
Lylakt Brush
Sky Landing
Break Plain
Yodh plateau
Raystronghold
Peace
Riv valley
Lamedh
Arimeth mountains
Nūn
Shyter
Ravenwoods
Passage of
Thela
Allrisen Mountains
Dravien Fortress
Try Valley
Parched Mill
Heth Rivers
Serifinoc wood
Kyr
Alpin forest
Arithmere Plain
Ykr
Aramithia woods
Aleph Plain
Myth Plateau
Rav Stronghold
Tiren Stream
Shin forest
Kaph Plateau
Ever Passage
Clevyk woods
Jagged falls
Passage Mountains
Small Plain
Guardian Mountains
Feather Plain
Riv
Gethsemani Mounts
Clearing forest
Ryerry
Nithyh forest
Ayint
Ayint wood
Disappearing River
Armour Rivers
Sparce woods
Zylon Plain
Lackt
Kyr Plain
Coryn Plain
Silent forest
Rallandys Pools
Zazlyn Tributaries
Nacēva Ocean

Argdrak
Locklynvalley
Dragon plateau
Claw Rivers
Arundel
Resting forest
Peppering Mounts
Paramour
Parched River
Bryak Plain
Neveah
Neveah Springs
Cloud-cover woods
Arbitrating Plain
Cyndere Plain
Autumnwood
Cyvyr
Windless wood
Sunlit Expanse
Key Mountains
Key
Coryander Plateau
Vanishing outlet
Groaning forest
Lyre Gap
Eversmiry
Stronghold
Passage Mounts
Fortress
The Red Plain
Terrago
Pine forest
Yintuar Ocean
Misty plateau
Illuruins
Crossmounts
Xerair woods
Isen foothills
Zyy plain
Nyros
Tethmarsh
Sycamore forest
Dwinding Mounts
Vyst wood
Forbidden fortress
Esgaroth
Rivensky
Broken River
Byrkenheights
Rivelwood
Qithiruins
Ykr Plain
Unnamed Region

Eloquent Books
An imprint of AEG Publishing Group
845 Third Avenue, 6th Floor – 6016
New York, NY 10022
www.eloquentbooks.com

ISBN: 978-1-60693-587-3 1-60693-587-9

Printed in the United States of America

Table of Contents

Ch. 0 The Existence Of A Rider's Egg page 11
Ch. 1 The Beginning Of A Sense Of Adventure page 14
Ch. 2 Syfrin page 20
Ch. 3 Warrior's Light In A Destiny page 25
Ch. 4 Ints page 34
Ch. 5 Arqyn page 38
Ch. 6 Xavier page 43
Ch. 7 Blade's End page 47
Ch. 8 Zayin The Warrior page 52
Ch. 9 Two Destinies Collide page 56
Ch. 10 Ablaze page 60
Ch. 11 All In A Cloth page 63
Ch. 12 Seven page 66
Ch. 13 A Foe Of A Friend page 70
Ch. 14 The Growl That Broke The Mountains page 77
Ch. 15 Heart Of A Dragon page 82
Ch. 16 Escape page 86
Ch. 17 Rivers Of Armour page 89
Ch. 18 Hope In A Stone page 92
Ch. 19 Awake page 95
Ch. 20 The First Flame page 98
Ch. 21 Pure Fire page 101
Ch. 22 Channel Of Memories page 105
Ch. 23 By Blood page 111
Ch. 24 Standing On Air page 115
Ch. 25 Chance In A River page 118
Ch. 26 Visible Air page 121
Ch. 27 Focusing On Wind page 124
Ch. 28 One Thousand To Five Thousand page 126
Ch. 29 Ryden A Cur page 129
Ch. 30 Sacrifice In A Word page 134
Ch. 31 The Long Awaited Blue Flame page 137
Ch. 32 A Window To The Clash Of Worlds page 140

Introduction

Hello reader!

I am so excited that you chose this story to read. What an honor it is of mine to know that my book is in your hand as you reveal its contents with your eyes. My only hope is that you sincerely enjoy it.

In this section, I am supposed to tell you a little bit about what I've learned on this journey toward becoming an author, and what an elating journey that is…instead, I think I'll write a little bit of encouragement to the reader and the aspiring writer:

To the reader: dream very big, for your aspiration can come true with hard work. Let your mind soar through these pages for a time, wandering about through the realms of Esgaroth, Terranith, and so on. Just remember to let your mind wander and conjure your imaginative curiosity; let your speculations take flight on this new venture, and never look backward.

To the aspiring author, I write: if you really love it, then do it (with an unhindered spirit in the clutches of your fingers). Don't worry about what the finished papers will look like or even how choppy the words will come at first. A story sometimes ends unexpectedly with nowhere to go and nothing to expound upon…Don't worry about that either; that's just a part of writing: soon, you'll be getting along in a story that you can't help but finish. Don't think…That's the trick…Don't think, but write. Curious phrase, yes, but use these little scribbles on the pieces of your imagination to make something come alive. That's what writing is: capturing a phrase and turning it into your own "something", where the reader can see your descriptions as if they were as crisp as an article laid before their very eyes. Let these words take on the very nature they possess, without letting their wild and unbroken meaning be as their opposites. Leave room for uncertainty to cloud your gaze for a moment. Then, find your way out of the ambiguous air in which you find yourself and your characters entrapped. Nothing is impossible: with God especially (for that's truly how anything is possible)…Why, I say this with experience, even if I am a mere 17 years of age. Impossibility is my favorite word. When there's impossibility, there is always going to be speculation; it always accompanies impossibility. Then, the impossibility reasons out into something palpable and even tangible, like an existent ray of sun. You can feel it, so it's real. But, can you catch it? That's the question. Catching sunlight: an eye captures sunlight, captivates it, and manipulates it into an availing sight for one's senses. I may just be rambling here, but nothing is quite as sweet as the expectations set upon the shoulders of impossibility.

To the aspiring writer: don't be afraid of what others think of your work…Or be afraid; either one. But, respect something first: the "equitability" for change lies in the hands of the writer alone. What was that prose? "No one can make you feel inferior without your consent" (Eleanor Roosevelt). Same principle here. Yes, it's true.

To those who can't think of anything "good" to write; who the judge of good and bad in this aspect is solely yourself: set down the pen for a time, or the pencil: for those who are feeling left out, you pencil people, (and the typers) and step away from the paper for a while. Hard to do…Now that we have you three separated, observe. One word with a grander meaning, so let me elaborate a moment. Watch something, whether it be entity or article; animal or natural phenomenon: not that glowing box (horrible). See it, and turn it over in your mind. When you touch it and feel it becoming yours, develop the spectacle into a long, winding, descriptive sentence (not too descriptive: no one likes too much description, but we'll get to that later). For now, be as detailed and descriptive as you see fit. Write, my friend, for that is a good "soul on paper" (Mary T. Lane). Write and listen to the strokes slide across the manuscript, an indescribable sound that makes a great joy stir into the fingers from the heart (the heart first, the head last: that's where the editing comes in).

For this is where the journey begins. Write…Don't aspire: but be.

But truly, I have learned a great many things through this opportunity: one is that you cannot hide your gifts, no matter how hard you try to conceal them away from others (especially if they have the potential, and they do, to give glory to the One who gave you these gifts). No matter how small this talent of writing, I hope it can bring God glory. And that's the truth: the Lord of lords is the only One worthy of receiving the recognition and credit, not myself!

Enjoy the reading!

Taylor J. Beisler

0

The Existence Of A Rider's Egg

Hear it crashing upon you; closing your eyes, you hear it- the sound that changed the course of this realm. The icy mantle yields its fraying mist, breaking as it goes, now rushing so succinctly upon your bare feet, drawing them down into the grainy earth. Then, the wave expires back into the rimy mountains and thalassic hills from whence it came. You hear it again as the sea pulses, trammeling you in its very nature of sound. The resounding gongs of the ocean cling to your senses, as they seem to be the rustling of a hand underneath the breadth of a great blanket, drawing it forth and back again. The wind finds you as it slows down and rushes through time, as a woe taking every breath by the reins. You open your eyes as you see the pulse dithering through the sea; the wave of invisible fluctuations runs after the throb of luminescent light, scampering across the horizon. The beat crashes against you, knocking the very breath away from your grasp as the pulses increase in speed, the surroundings slowly ceasing to sift into existence. You close your eyes, hardly able to breathe as the unimaginable occurs, the prospect considering how it used to ring so clearly. Then, all is still. All is silent. Your eyes crack, now shy of the gleaming light that is so strange to your glance; as the rays pierce your eyes, you direct your gaze downward upon the halted shore of polar reflections. A stone lay, caressed by the hands of fate, lingering amidst the pearled flits of light emanating from its internal. The entity seems to have been formed by this strange phenomenon, but is it real? Is it tangibly existent? You crouch, balancing your hands expertly out as to lay your fingers on the article, but something holds you back. You look up and see that the scene is crumbling into view, beholding darkness as the light. There's nothing but you, the stone, the ancient secret, and silence. The stone remains, waxing by the now reflecting breaks in the sky. Somewhere, a rider was born, and his thoughts formed the last egg that would ever be, like a wave cultivating a shell by its pure, gleaming rush. You are torn away from this scene, left with naught but a memory. Or is it only so simple?

Now the reader has to take the first action in this journey. Should you flip the page, there is no turning back.

1

The Beginning Of A Sense Of Adventure

"Mom! No…get off! Mom …"

The wavering voice belonged to a small boy, his eyes blue with tears, and his hair silver, as his Shilen background prevailed.

"No …"

His small features disappeared from her sight; his very being was wrenched from her.

"My child! No, my boy…my husband…Phasen …" her small voice trailed off, as she was being held by ropes and swords under the influence of a guard.

His high cheekbones were now scathed raw, meeting the ground harshly, as a sentry dragged the boy, carrying him and his father; he didn't know where.

"Dad? …"

His beautiful eyes gave way to a tear, which he wiped away by his tightly tied hands.

"Dad, is mom gonna be okay?"

His breathing drew to a jagged end as it revealed his sadness.

His father had brown, sparkling eyes always full of optimism. And with his hands wrapped in chains, he looked back at his son.

"My boy, she's going to be fine …"

He cupped his fingers and brushed his son's chin gingerly.

"They're not going to do anything to your mother." And with that, he looked away as a silent tear fled his eye, covering the truth from his son.

"I promise you: wherever we're going, we'll be okay; you know that...I always love you, my boy."

His father's slim face, which was brutally beaten by the Syfrin, smiled despondently into the boy's glistening view.

"Xavier?"

The boy's eyes alighted at his name as he felt the pressure from his father's fingers tighten underneath his chin, guiding his focus onto the sad figure beside him.

"You believe me?"

His father's gentle whisper became enough as Xavier replied, "Yes, sir."

A tear wound down his cheek as he pursed his lips to keep another from falling.

"Nyros! Your only hope!" laughed a patrol as he threw them, together with many other boys and men, against the walled pathway.

"Dad ..."

His look told his father of his fear.

"It's all right, Xavier ..."

His large hands cradled the boy; Xavier was now trembling uncontrollably, trying to be as brave as he could appear.

"You!"

A guard pointed a grave hand in his father's direction as Xavier began to protest, fumbling over his feet to stand.

"Boy, don't test me-"

The Syfrin hit Xavier with his hilt, sending him recoiling back into the ground.

"No!"

His father stood between Xavier and the sentinel as he continued, "Don't hurt the boy; take me ..."

Xavier's face became nothing short of horrified, as his sullen father was led like a lamb to the slaughter.

"Dad ..."

Xavier managed to reach his small, gnarled hand on the pathway to try to hold them back; a tear streamed down his face, and his breathing wavered.

§

It was one of those days where the wind felt crisper than ever before, and the indescribable scent of adventure came about. It was one of those days where a spark of discovery would seem to come upon you and grasp you by the shoulders, yanking you away from the very road set under your feet. It was when time had no merit, and miracles were still alive. It was when the hand of the enemy was moving quickly.

His name was Airsing. He had handsome features, although usually musty with dirt and soot from his tool work. His dark, blue eyes seemed to drink in everything. His hair was a light russet, with a few strands of dark brown finding glimpses of his eyes.

Before us now, his hair stands and flees from the sparks of the fire as he looks up for a moment, evidently transfiguring the piece of metal in his hands to an object worthy to hold someone's deference.

There was something indescribably different about him; not that he had one pointed ear or anything of the sort. Yes, his character was different in nobility, but something else; he never felt he belonged. He was a key, the type of key that seemed worn and lost to something of great purpose, that fit somewhere else. He wanted to be in a different world, where every second seemed like a new adventure, where he could breathe.

"Airsing! Good to see your sparks flying this morning!"

"Hey, grandfather. What's up for today?" he heard his voice perk up at the rough tone.

"We have three repairs: a shearer, a shovel, and an iron clasp …" his intonation faded on the last part, "one metal work and a few shoes…Tolkien wants you to make one of your swords."

"Unusual, I wonder what he's going to use it for?" he mumbled, intending the question for himself, rhetorical.

"He didn't say."

Airsing's grandfather perused the notes he scratched onto pieces of paltry parchment; he had already started to hum the tune he had perfected so many days ago.

"Well, let's go, then; I've already gotten the wood."

"You were alive *this* morning."

He heartily brushed Airsing's shoulder as he stooped to swipe up a few pieces of the kindling.

Airsing set his hammer down as he fed the timber into the sparking fire, which was now swallowing every inch of bark in the flitting lights. He clutched a cloth and wiped his musty hands, as well as the blade of the stiletto he was using to punch a hole in a saddle for a makeshift dee ring and stirrups. He took a second and pushed his palms onto the table, fond of his deepening thoughts.

They were too poor to afford coal, but wood suited them just as well. Besides, Airsing's swords were some of the best in the region.

After a few turns and sparks, a familiar object appeared in the fire: a blade. He stood humbly testing the edges and tip with his thumb, licking his tainted fingers in approval.

The day fled quickly under the hands of the blacksmith. He looked up every once and a while to watch the birds or the leaves in the forest next to the forge.

I wonder what ever got me here ... he began, setting his metal work down and snatching up the musty cloth, kneading it in-between his strong hands.

Arousing his melancholic thoughts, the door's familiar crack expelled them from his mind. Upon seeing his grandfather start to measure for a repair, he turned and climbed nimbly through the wobbly stairs, as he had done many times before. He appeared into a finely furnished room, or so it was to the eyes of a blacksmith: with walls ornamented with tools of every kind, displaying their work prudently to the straying eye.

At first he didn't see anyone, until his gaze was set a hair shorter to a humble figure.

"Hello, son. I'm getting ready to close up for today, but before I do…I was wondering if the sword is ready?"

The man's eyes turned to small moons as his glasses slid onto the edge of his nose; Airsing was now seeing him rustle them back upon their perch.

Tolkien was a short, stocky man of about his grandfather's age. His white hair peppered what had been his head of light brown, which was mostly bald except for the back that was usually concealed by a brown, tarnished hat.

With a, "Yes, sir, one moment," Airsing returned with sword in hand, dusting the edges so it would shine; cascading lights danced across the ivory gleams of the newly fashioned blade. He threw the rag aside as he handed the spectacle to the admirer.

"Fine work you do, Master Airsing…fine work. I thank you so much, son."

Tolkien examined the sword, eyes opening wider, then squinting as to take in every detail. He was now tilting back his head to see through his glasses that had slowly begun to regress to their favored spot.

"Seems I've misplaced-" his eyes faded as he felt his pockets, his brow furrowing as to stifle his next sentence.

"Sir?"

Airsing muscled through the scraps and tools on the worn tabletop to uncover a box, all the while keeping his eyes on Tolkien.

"Oh, nothing. Here's the price, I believe. I'll even put in a few more."

His countenance masked his attitude cleverly as he held the sword, walking out from the tool shop.

Upon closing the small box and latching it, simultaneously walking toward the forge, Airsing's eyes groped along a ridged object. Its unique glimmer justified the small, yet curious article; a package lay just beside it, as if it had fallen from the envelope.

He gathered the entity quickly up into the package and hastily caught Tolkien almost by the scarf as a rush of cold wind scarred his face, contrasting greatly with the warmth of the forge's fire.

"Sir," Airsing's words were directed toward Tolkien, though they trailed off to meet the ears of the wind.

Tolkien, now hunkering over to prevent the frosty gusts, turned quickly to see the discolored package in Airsing's strong, left hand.

"I found this-"

Tolkien took it quickly from Airsing without saying a word, though staring at him nonetheless. His eyes faded, as he finally had to reveal the story behind the countenance so earlier known as his façade.

"This dragon scale belonged to my father who inherited it from his, and so the story goes ..." his voice crept lower as he grasped the object tighter, crumpling it away from sight into his weathered coat pocket.

As he began to feel the sincerity of his voice, Airsing itched his nose with the tip of his nail as he was now clutching the loose-knit shirt rashly ruffled about his lean frame.

"The last dragon that ever lived." Tolkien smiled slightly at the thought with a disheartening sigh, "…But that was a long time ago."

Tolkien reflected for a moment, then his countenance deepened in thought as he lifted his eyes.

"Dark times are coming, Airsing. Be cautious and with you the light will not be quenched."

He held his gaze on the young man standing before him; he was not yet tarnished with age or by time, but more by soot than anything else, though not molded directly by it.

With his last words, Tolkien ran down the hill as Airsing stopped for a moment before returning to the musty snare of the forge that so entrapped him. He looked down onto his left hand, at most and at the same time, at least, hoping for something to happen.

The chilling wind flew through his hair as his mind escaped into Tolkien's words:

Be cautious and with you the light will not be quenched.

2

Syfrin

As his scarred hands etched the mark into the wall, finger lifting to run along the etchings: *yep…fifteen years* had passed to the day. His hair now black and his eyes impeccably imbrued red, he had become like one of them. It was in their words, actions, thoughts, food, and even their water. He remembered little, but was sure it was still there because of an evidently persistent tug on the back of his mind. His nature became hard and unyielding as the two sides of him grew carefully detached, though each fought for their own, solitary existence.

Just the other day he had seen what had been left of his father. The only similarity he remembered was the placing of his features; nothing remained. They had taken Phasen and beaten him into a Syfrin.

Every few days, Xavier heard news of life outside the dank walls of his cell; from this he quickly gathered that his father was the commander of King Arkt's army, the ones who had transformed them with the vile natures they now possessed.

Every time he saw his father, nothing good came of the encounter to say the least; Xavier got beaten, threatened, and tormented by what was left of his phantom.

He held as fast as he could to the memories of the truth: his father as respectable and right, but nothing seemed to stick for long. A faint tear now resonated of his past Shilen sensation of sorrow, an emotional eclipse that he was growing more and more calloused toward; the globule fled from sight, as he quickly wiped it away.

He diverted his mind to other things as he looked about his all too familiar surroundings: the cell ran upward until it met the cobblestone, reaching a great, round opening that the stars would shine down through, but the sun could never seem to find.

He discovered that his Shilen likeness was becoming less and less worth the time and even harder than he had thought to keep; he tried everything he could, but the greatest thing that prevailed was taking care of the few animals he found crawling into his cell.

His mind stopped as he closed his eyes; he seemed to be drowning in the silence of knowing that his thoughts were concealed.

Suddenly, he heard unfamiliar hooves echoing and banging off the stones inside his cell. As he cupped the back of his head in his hands, he stationed himself against the hollow of the wall where he could hear what was happening.

Guards squabbled and clashed their armor together until one piped up: "An Arqyn?! That's it? Not some boy …"

A whisper incomprehensible, then: "What?! I thought you said he was skilled…He failed at the attack? Oh, sure: white sparks are just that, a firework…What do you think?" his voice madly trailed off in the other direction as his tirade continued.

"Boy!" a gruff tone began as it scraped at the door's keyhole, opening the wretched cell into the morning air.

The guard yanked Xavier, now known as Ÿr, into the strange land. The dark and light seemed to have no difference in this infested area.

As Ÿr shook his hands free from bondage, massaging his gashed wrists, he peered woefully around, taking in the grotesque setting of cobblestone and dark, forest trees. The trees grew as tall as the tower set before him, which was camouflaged with cracked shadows; the very bark and stone seemed to loom with the infirmity prevalent in all the inhabitants.

As the guard jerked him down stairs and through passageways, he felt a groping silence that made him uneasy.

The sentry's grip wrenched Ÿr's gashed wrists as they maneuvered around the sharp corners, falling deeper into the evil chambers. The sentinel took a moment's peace, yanking Ÿr backward; the Syfrin then proceeded into a corridor with lights shedding naught but darkness into the bleak hall.

As they turned another corner, he recognized the emaciated form of his father. Jolting pain now seized Ÿr as he felt his knees buckle underneath of him, the guard planting his face into the ground and then releasing him. His ankles were weak from the shackles, so it took him a long time to muster his strength to stand.

"Sun's shadow …" his father contemplated, "Take him to the captives...."

He threw a bucket and brush into Ÿr's hands and motioned him from the room, as a few cackled their approval of his treatment.

Ÿr was given many tasks: from equipping men and horses to cleaning stalls. He also aided the army in strategies, as he would fight with the Syfrin to train them for battle. He found the first time he held a sword awkward, but caught on quickly as he grew to acknowledge this great necessity: if he didn't, it would mean the end of his life, as he was the only one lacking the protection of armor.

He gained an arch nemesis out of an, now steady, int by the name of Duma, who couldn't catch his quick blade. Duma suspected him as having more than a dark side to him.

§

The sun climbed through the trees, hanging and tripping over the boughs as the blinding light was now free from the length of their barky arms; one pale ray met Airsing's back as he skulked through the sullen branches and leaves of the new, crisp layer set before him.

Every step seemed to reveal his presence in the lightening forest. Smoke fled his nostrils as he peered toward the river, fog rising from the surface. As he slowed his steps, a persisting sound was uncovered by the silence.

Airsing carefully swerved, surveying the place where he had heard the noise; nothing.

As he studied the signs of the forest, he resolved to wait patiently in a crevice. Sure enough, a crack, then a long shoo, crack. The dragging elongated until it came to a halt; more cracks.

Wanting to be heard, a blade hit the very interface between Airsing and the metal.

If he stalled, if he ran: there was no time to grasp the cause and effect of the action. Airsing sprinted into the forest as fast as his feet would carry him, tripping slightly from takeoff on the dew-laden leaves.

He knew the sound: Syfrin. The foe was quickly following, masked as the trees and shadows.

I know where you are, Airsing, son of Soren.

His mind raced as his pace quickened even more until he noticed the absence of ground beneath his feet; air filled the grass that used to lie underneath his step. A claw-like grip tightened on his arm, sharp as nails through wood.

He couldn't see anything; everything was blurred as the wind rushed through his hair.

You are the one I've been searching for, Airsing, the voice quietly whispered in words, though not clear.

He couldn't speak; he tried, but all he uttered were the words: "Arin eth te uth ran kiren."[1]

These words were legendary, yet not to his knowledge.

You know who I am, Airsing ... the different tongue flooded his mind.

Abruptly, his feet found a solid landing as his knees allowed for recoil, palms meeting the forest brush. He stood quickly as he felt a warm, powerful rush of wind hit his neck.

His eyes sought his enemy's face as he turned; there was no living thing behind him. He glanced into the darkness of the path from whence he had fallen; a chilling wind rustled the leaves along the floor, but that was it.

What are you looking for?

A bright pair of eyes met his brow as he swerved, ready for a fight; he was holding his stiletto, used more for finishing his blacksmith work than anything else, subtly out of view, taken aback by the creature standing majestically before him. The sun seemed to delight itself in touching the tips of the reflective, white scales jaggedly portrayed in this spectacle.

---

[1]Literal meaning: To kill a sword is given.

The whiteness of the eyes surrounded a surreal greenness, which changed in brightness. They captured his senses for a moment and then released him.

He quietly took a step backward as he surveyed the sharp flecks that ran down the creature's back, once more noticing their clarity in the blinding hue of white that transgressed the very reality of a color's true intensity.

You are Airsing, am I right? These woods are not safe, especially for you. You know of the Syfrin and their doing.

The creature, once again, penetrated his mind.

Lumos, tir a treer arint saratir.[2]

The beast's own tongue was revealed as if by this one sentence.

You are my rider, Airsing. The time has come ...

He stuck out his hand to feel the scales on her snout, finding she was more real than he could have ever imagined.

"*Your* rider?"

Yes. I chose you long before I was alive. In this age, Rider, the Xav are allying once again with the ints and Syfrin. They are going to muster an army larger than any force before them...They are seeking vengeance for their leader. If we don't fight them, this age will be lost to darkness, and that ray of light will become nothing but a reflection of what could've been.

When they killed each rider and dragon, one by one, at Rivensky, the last hopes to perish darkness were quenched.

---

[2] Literal meaning: Warrior's Light (see footnote 5), you are the dragon rider.

3

Warrior's Light In A Destiny

Ÿr perused his aching knees as his pensive mind took flight on a new venture to keep his thoughts from fleeing too much toward the pain. He groaned inwardly as he relaxed his tight muscles slightly against the wall; his brow was still chilled with blood.

"Boy!"

He looked up to see his father standing like a vulture in the doorway, which sprung open on command.

"Bring the chain," he enjoined as he turned his companion away from the cell door.

"'is witss, too …" the Xav commented.

Ÿr picked up the chain, resting forebodingly in the corner, and followed. He never spoke, yet only when he was alone to keep himself resolute and sane. The most words he had ever heard were echoing through his thoughts, where he lingered as they journeyed to a grave place, solemn and deepening in gloom. He crept silently upon the scene, handing the chain to his father; Ÿr cringed at the thought of this man as his once noble father.

A Shilen likeness now filled his view as Ÿr kept vigil; he was curious to see one of his own kind, previous own kind anyway. The man's eyes were full of something like a light that Ÿr couldn't explain, even under coercion.

"You won't tell us where it is…just like your stupid son!"

Ÿr's father stepped upon the prospect, playfully writhing the chain in and out of his loose grip.

As he kicked the Shilen to the cold floor, he lowered his head to the ground and whispered something to the man, as a long, unsettling growl permeated the air; the Shilen's brow furrowed, though he didn't say a word as he directed his gaze upward.

"Ledyneer…who do you think you're messing with?"

Ÿr's father wrapped the chain around the man's neck, as he withheld nothing from the torture he so enjoyed giving.

A sorcerer now crept slyly into the room with a monstrous creature behind him. Nothing could describe this immortal beast. Ÿr hid behind a column as his eyes inched out, settling upon the creature. It seemed the being could sense whatever difference there was between the good in the Shilen and the evil in the Syfrin by even the slightest intimation from a sniff or even by sight.

"We'll make this simple …"

A Syfrin motioned for the thing.

As the sorcerer stepped aside, the Syfeklen, or so they called it, screeched and turned a horrible shape as it lunged for the man. Ÿr turned his eyes away as he was now pinned against the wall by the shrill shriek, which spun him around the stairs; the grieving growl rang mercilessly throughout his thoughts, scattering even the easiest of tasks, such as standing, into nothing but confusion. He was now unstably trying to steady himself until he tumbled over onto the ground. He lifted up his head as paces resounded almost upon him; all the air in his lungs evaporated. His focus dripped quickly into a pool of torturous eyes, as he couldn't move; he was frozen to his place as the creature slowly diverted away from him by means of the sorcerer's words.

"Maybe that'll do him good: insolent fool …" his father trailed off as he now became the catalyst for all the murmurs in-between.

Ÿr hurriedly scurried up and was orderly kicked against the wall, where he blacked out.

§

Crack …

"What was that?"

Syfrin.

"How did you keep hidden?"

Airsing's eyes were now drinking in the awe of his reality.

Like this.

The creature bowed her forewing.

In a split instant, they were above the trees, seeing sky as far as the eye could acquire.

"This is amazing ..."

He lifted his arms, only to catch her forewings as he found the stress from the wind was greater than he had envisaged.

Yes, you'll get used to it.

"What's your name…how do you know mine?" his voice seemed to trail away, emulating the day he had talked to Tolkien.

Young warrior, you have much to learn. My name is Syocer…and how I know yours: I was created by the sense. I know where you are and can find your thoughts.

"Then, I don't have to ask you my next question."

His features ravenously imbibed the cold breeze as he whipped his hair away from his wandering eyes.

Yes, I'd like to hear it. I don't want to come into your mind like your enemy. That will come soon enough with trust...As your kind say: you must aim before you shoot, yes?

"Oh…sure …" he whispered, weighing the reply, "Why me, then?"

His eyes were directed upward, yet were focusing on his peripheral.

Because of your character…simple enough. I see you have great integrity and a heart worthy of trust. If you look around, there's not too many you can say that about. You also have a thirst for adventure…I can help there.

"When is the war you were talking about…or an indication of some kind…when is it supposed to, you know," he tried to think of the right word as it appeared directly into his thoughts, "…happen?"

Some say over a course of a few years, a battle here and there. Some say there will be one then another ...

Just then, a huge burst of white sparks precipitately fled into the air a few leagues ahead of them.

Must be earlier than I've imagined. Rider, be quick on your feet. I'll be waiting for you.

Before he could speak, Syocer dropped Airsing onto the tattered and tried frame now underneath his palms. He scurried down, climbing into the cloth-covered opening as he hastily gathered lasting elements for food. He stopped suddenly as his gaze trickled over to the edge of the room, where his grandfather was poised asleep in his wooden chair. Airsing held the sac closed with one hand as he evaded the creaks in the wooden floor. He stationed his foot on the aperture, but hesitated slightly as he swung the bag over his shoulder. He looked toward his grandfather; Airsing's feelings were moving too quickly for decisiveness when Syocer breached his thoughts.

Don't; if you stay for a moment more, they'll find you.

He grabbed a water cask as he climbed out from the melancholy structure. He jumped, meaning to hit the ground, as Syocer flew beneath him; he caught her fleeting tail by the scales as it flew by nonchalantly.

Good job. Not many riders can do that, she laughed, all too fond of jest.

He gripped her tail as his already calloused hands started to bleed into blisters.

Come up, Airsing. Hurry, on my back. We have a long way to travel in a short time.

Airsing gradually detached and reattached himself from scale to scale until he came up on her back wings.

"Well, that was interesting…hardly would have imagined flying feels like this …"

He leaned on her wing, which threw her unexpectedly spiraling through the wind.

Airsing tried to reach for something steady to grasp, but found nothing surer than air as he fled into the blue of the sky, Syocer rushing after him.

As he was about to rivet into the ground, his whole being felt a simple word: *Syrelynt.*[3]

His vision halted, fixing on Syocer's still rapid movements as his eyes felt the surroundings. His form was still; not a hair on his head moved, as it froze in the split instant the word was breathed into existence.

Syocer reached for his arm as she ascended with a quick reaction of her wings, soaring in svelte agility.

Kï.[4]

---

[3] Literal meaning: Still.

His body flooded with vivacity as his numb hands tingled with feeling.

"What happened?" he gasped as his chest felt the pressure of the altitude once more, now grateful for the stress on his breath.

You have unlocked a piece of you that has been destined to be so ...

After he had recovered his senses, he studied the terrain beneath Syocer's scales.

"So, the tongue you speak, is it-?"

An old Rader language: dragons and riders used it to keep out any invading thoughts so no one could understand what the one said to the other. Each dialect has words equal and different for each rider and dragon.

"Lumos?"

Yes. Airsing is as Lumos[5].

He lingered upon Syocer's back, now flat against her, as mountains filled his gaze; he no longer knew where they were, as his mind foraged for answers.

Syocer sensed the growing curiosity of the young man on her back as she began; a map as clear as the lands themselves appeared in his thoughts:

To the mountains of Raromere, king of Alrisen, we go past the rivers of Armour, through the passage of Erev, and by the woods of Aramithia.

"Amazing, how did you-" as he was speaking, the map disappeared as easily as it had been conjured.

You will find that each dragon and rider is given different talents. If used, many are uncovered.

†

As soon as he came to, he heard his father speaking to a general about reasons of a certain "war". He became aware of his position: in a corner by a table peering up through the cracks in the

---

[4] Literal meaning is uncertain, though used in this context as: Become or Energy.

[5] Literal meaning has never been truly discovered till this day, but has been thought of as being: Warrior's Light or as "Key to" something, though never truly deciphered as to what.

knotting wood. He gingerly rubbed the back of his head, which he felt was wet. He drew his hand back and sure enough, there was the blood. He now studied upon the wooden sky.

"This…this can be unlocked by the destined Arqyn!"

"War! Keep your head straight!…The Xav are planted at Rivensky …"

"And the siege on the Arqdrak city? A base, I presume?"

The silence appeared to be the general's head nodding and some drawings on a map.

Ÿr's eyes were now squinting, in part to keep himself from giving breath to his pain and also as a means to converge his thoughts.

"Our army will have to reinforce here …"

"And Sant Key?"

Before they could finish their conversation, a crack rang inexorably throughout the tower as it clambered upon their now rigid frames.

"The Syfeklen has been restless these last days …"

Footsteps crept upon the scene as the owner of the steps whispered a command in their confidence.

"They've found the dragon in the sky?"

"Yes, sir, we have watch on the four winds …"

At the word "dragon", Ÿr focused ardently through the table's cracks, though all he could see was a cloth held in-between two stones, intending his sight to fall upon the messenger; he had only heard of such a fable, as a dragon, in stories.

"Take the boy to his cell!" ordered his father as quickly as the messenger had taken flight from the room.

Ÿr relaxed his neck muscles, forgetting his aching head; he cringed, but quickly realigned his features as he became, apparently, lifeless.

As he was being dragged, unbound because of his "livid" state, he looked around and took in the eerie safety, if you can call it such a thing, of his plan. He dug his palms into the ground and found strength enough to stop the force that pulled him across the path. Upon looking back, the guard dropped the young man and inspected the scene. And in that moment, Ÿr jumped up and covered the Syfrin's mouth, wrestling him to the ground. And taking the Syfrin's knife, Ÿr knocked the sentry unconscious as he drew him to his own cell. Tying the sentinel and sheathing the red blade, he picked up a bow from the armory and crept around undetected.

He made his way through the ducts back toward the extent he had previously inhabited under the table; he found that the scope was still occupied by the cloth, though no other entity.

Ÿr quickly snatched the material, figuring it was of some importance, and fled from the room.

Just then, shadows came dancing across the stairway, trying to catch the noise of the clanking steps resounding before them. Ÿr jolted behind a column as he flattened himself against it, pressuring his ears to pick up on any sign that acknowledged he had escaped.

"Oedyas…still guarding the door, I see…."

The voices dithered across the height of the tower as Ÿr looked down upon the article in his hands, now relaxing a bit. As he examined the feathery material, he saw a strange mark on the side, as if it had been exposed to fire. The burn-like section appeared to unmask some sort of symbols. He resolved that it needed to be fully immersed in flames as he slipped it away from sight, realizing now that the shadows had escaped his relaxed wariness.

He quietly inched out into the cascading lights that broke through the cracking structure, bringing with them particles of pollen that rained down upon the silent darkness of the extent.

He made it back down to a courtyard that was encircled by a deserted stable, with the exception of some horses. And upon finding a horse, he set out to find this "Arqyn", though whether to kill him or not was still a great phantom in his mind.

Xavier brushed off his new name as he unsaddled the horse in the far-off woods. He would soon come across many obstacles, now that the Syfrin in his cell had just been found, and the general had presently discovered the cloth missing from the room. They would be in quick pursuit and would need a diversion. He threw the horse's saddle and all throughout the woods as he unbridled the animal to make the journey quicker and lighter; he tugged the last rope tied to the arc of his horse's snout, his feet stumbling on every step. He threw the small particles of food that he had just managed to muster, fumbling to keep a few bits as he threw the others resentfully away from his position. Finding that there was nothing left to hinder their journey, he drew his blade and cut down a few branches in the next path, fastening pieces of clothing along the sticks protruding from the brush; all the while, his eyes were excitedly rummaging through the pages of the forest as to detect a straying foe.

He looked backward, then tugged at the horse's rope as he jumped onto its back, escaping the scene; the Syfrin appeared there only minutes later.

As Xavier galloped through the woods, he found it interesting that his int-like nature was struggling to hold on as it kept catching his mind, threatening to leave forever.

As the ride lengthened, he tried as hard as he could to yank his mind from his shadow; his spirit was now jaded from the battle, leaving lassitude as his only equitable reason (and temptation) to surrender.

He had been riding for a day straight and appeared on the Red Plain. He didn't know where to go, for he couldn't remember ever seeing anything outside of Nyros; Xavier was now moving more uncertainly than ever.

He stepped his horse into a good rate, though not directing the animal's paces.

After a good while, the horse lulled to a halt as Xavier decided that a rest would be fairly welcomed. He patted the beast on the neck as he looked around, jumping from the animal's back and leading his companion by the mane.

As he noticed his tongue dryly sticking to the roof of his mouth, he took a quick glance toward the horse, which snout seemed bitterly thirsty from its dry appearance. He knew nothing of how he could get water, until they heard the sound of heaven on earth: a stream. It was not so much the stream, but the misty pearls that rained from its surface, which had first engulfed them.

Bugs were flicking at the animal's eyes and back as it brushed them away phlegmatically; Xavier was now steadying himself on the soggy bank, trying to contain his thirst.

He cupped the cool water in his hands and showered the horse with the droplets as it whinnied at the refreshing bliss. The animal's nature then developed in solemnity as it dipped its chapped snout into the pool, drinking in the relief.

Xavier wrung his hands from the wet ground as he splashed the liquid on his face. He whipped his dripping hair away from his eyes as he patted the horse, pushing the animal's hungry sniffs carefully away from his head.

He fumbled upon a niche in the side of a mountain and decided that it would be a good place to rest, as he was now holding out a piece of bread to his dry lips. Xavier presented a small chunk to his companion as the horse smothered the piece with dribble, gratefully taking it from his hand. He quickly reached back into his sac, not withstanding the desire to wipe his sodden hand, but found his spirit sinking as his fingers stumbled upon only a few crumbs brushed about the sac cloth.

Xavier now watched his horse pertinently pick a good spot to graze, as he positioned himself more adamantly against the rock wall of the niche; Xavier quickly fell asleep.

§

Here is the gateway to the mountains.

Her eyes gleamed in the sun that peered out from a frosty cover of gray clouds, seeming to hold the very atmosphere above its shoulders.

As Airsing looked up, the former was revealed as a city built into a mountain of stone with waterways, passages, and walls built almost as high as the mountain itself.

4

Ints

As Syocer clutched the rocks and dirt in her talons, Airsing hesitantly climbed from her back.

Don't be anxious...No one has ever seen a creature, like myself, in this place before...Though, I warn you: keep a careful guard on your tongue, for words can be the most treasured of persuasions. There are not too many whose hearts have yet strayed, though you can never be too cautious; the age is young.

She nudged him along, working against his stiff, scarred legs.

Immediately as the two met the gate, the watchman called, "State your name, Rider!"

"Airsing, son of Soren ..." Airsing looked involuntarily upward to see the voice's source, but his eyes met only the rock walls.

"Why have you traveled this far, only to be rejected?"

Syocer quickly searched the man's strange temperament, where she saw an evil loomed about his soul; an int held onto him, a shadow.

(Let us take a moment here to describe the object of Syocer's intrigue. An int, or a shadow, is known as such because of its curious character. This creature, being the very interface between a certain race of person and the separate race of Syfrin, is the first step into the darkness of the manipulative grip of Nyros. The int is of an inquisitive nature because its race possesses a certain rebellious tone about it, giving the perfect reflection of the two sides of the person it condemns. The int can appear as certainly as you are able to see it, or it can vacillate between visibility and invisibility depending on its desire for you to perceive it as such instances.)

Lumos, mean what you say…Give him your Name.

"…Others call me Lumos…and, I assure you: I have not come to get nowhere."

The very air seemed stunned, freezing in his breath as the gate split open across the view.

Syocer gingerly pushed Airsing through the creaking gates as his eyes leaned upon the tall mechanisms; his gaze now met the noisy streets before them, full of life and colorful aspects.

Every child, woman, man, and animal stared in awe of this spectacle as Airsing's feet echoed Syocer's path, her talons coolly clutching the earth.

Every trodden stone seemed miles underfoot as they met the end of the road, which was adorned aptly by the mountain passage in front of them, engulfing the very breath from their lungs. Syocer calmly led into the stifling air of the channel.

As the light faded inside the mountain, so did Airsing's vision.

Focus, Airsing...Draw in the light of your eyes …

He touched the dank walls, dripping with the tangible existence of darkness, as he paused. Airsing felt strained in a certain aspect, but he couldn't grasp from where the idea of this very thought was coming. He flexed his vision, pushing through the misty silence, as an object appeared to be scorning the very touch of his eyes; a small glimmer of smoke rose again as it covered up the sign of sight. He steadied himself on the hazy uncertainty for a moment, then reapplied himself to the force that engulfed him for the few seconds he stood in its midst.

You need to look through the forces…Touch it.

Syocer's voice was so easily subduing to the intense darkness that Airsing began to feel a radiance flickering from his pupils, lighting the pathway.

"Wow," he murmured, hearing the droplets of his voice dance across the alcoves throughout the tunnel.

The light scampered across the knots in the wet bricks, uncovering all but signs of life.

You've found these senses are acute...We have a gift; we have to use it ...

Their steps now reverberated off the dank earth as the halls came to a dimly lit end.

"Here he comes," a gruff voice cut through the musty air.

"He was found?" in disbelief another followed the echo.

"I believe she found him," the first restated his position.

"If not, he might have been killed by now," a noble tone fled from the solitary room.

They are friends of the mountains...Keep a steady hand and a resolved brow ...

She brushed his hair into place with a puff from her mouth as her eyes bowed into his.

There you go. Here, I'll lead you.

The weak light, once so newly disclosed by the length of the passages, was quenched by the fullness of the room's glow.

Syocer crouched as she displayed her meek strength in folding her wings; Airsing followed her, arm falling from the rough ridges of her neck scales.

He cast his glance across the room as the brightness became more familiar to his eyes; he blinked and the once apparent light, emanating from himself, collapsed back into his pupils.

A handful of Dwarves occupied a small table, which was carefully set askew from the center pieces of shields and armor; some others leaned toward the walls, became apprehensive, or were scrupulously drinking in Syocer's presence.

"Go ahead and state your name," the gruff tone began, the owner of this voice's hard eyes cloaking his friendly nature.

Syocer's concentration raced across the room to a shadow as Airsing hesitated, feeling Syocer's edgy muscles as his own, "Airsing ..."

Syocer sensed an ominous darkness growing in the room.

Your real Name, Syocer propelled a warm wind into the air from her now opened mouth.

"...It's Lumos."

Syocer's grip detached itself from the rocks it had clutched so fixedly, her scales smooth once more; Airsing's nerves now involuntarily relaxed as he glanced in Syocer's direction.

He's gone.

"An admirable Name. Mine is Raromere…I was given the position as king of this realm…Do not be anxious," he cautiously uttered under his furrowing eyebrows, sensing the tension.

"We have had trouble with ints these past days."

King Raromere cast his thoughts into the air while he stood, as was the ancient custom of the Dwarves to welcome someone of high standing.

"Ints are younger and brighter forms of Syfrin. Not too much on killing, only tormenting. Although, you will run into a few who will take advantage of the opportunity if they get the chance."

Raromere's countenance developed in seriousness.

"I understand we have some sort of…well, a task." Airsing masked his curiosity as he rerouted the subject.

"Ah…A task it shall be. Though, you shall never fully understand its magnitude, as none of us will. Each day grows a greater evil that is ready …" Raromere listened, his voice trailing off into the eternal silence of the tunnels.

Syocer's muscles nurtured uneasiness as Airsing's did the same. Her eyes flickered in the dimming fires, disturbed by the restlessness now overtaking the caverns.

An army.

5

Arqyn

Sunlight ran along his brow, lingering on his eyelashes as he awoke upon the scene of a lively dawn. He had never seen anything more beautiful in his life, as he remembered how sunlight once warmed his bones. He squinted horribly at first, but then grew used to the pleasant rays.

He readied his horse, which was now grazing on a very frugal, yet satisfying patch of milkweed.

Wary of their surroundings, they started toward the source of the river precariously, yet auspiciously set before them.

Then, Xavier heard a strange cracking, as if they were standing on a sheet of ice. He looked down and noticed that the ground was giving way underneath them. The horse bucked up on its hind legs as Xavier directed its hesitant steps away from the scene, its hooves now pawing the unsteady ground; they disappeared into the earth.

Xavier involuntarily jumped from his companion, reassuring himself that the animal's nimble ankles had gone without snapping. As he looked around, horse now spooked and standing, the trap didn't seem like much of one, as the thicket led into a dark, winding passage. Specks of light and long awaited dust now snowed upon their frames as Xavier looked upward. He seemed to be measuring how far they fell, meeting his palms together as the dusky dirt shed from his hands. A solution never met, they walked cautiously into the darkness as Xavier perked up at a long, rushing sound, as of a greater river running through these passages; the sound grew louder as they perused the darkness, stones starting to dribble toward their feet (and hooves).

As he came into a clearing, Xavier saw a faint light in the distance. The horse's breathing rapidly heaved as they inched forward. Xavier quietly muzzled its fright as he held onto its snout, now muddled by hispid hair and spit, and looked up into the spooked eyes of the horse. As he led them into the middle of the clearing, he noticed a wetness that had jumped upon him unexpectedly. It quickly drew them down through the rapids as his horse and he were washed away in the blink of an eye, Xavier covering the animal's eyes with what was left of his torn shirt.

§

"Airsing."

Raromere firmly stared into his eyes as to redirect his attention, "You have been given a great task despite its grave outlook. You have to take the responsibility of your Name."

Raromere reached for a piece of darkened parchment from the hand of a sac.

"Take this…a map. Find Zayin. He will know the rest."

He led an eye in Syocer's direction as the muted lights grazed the reflections of his sight.

"We'll hold off the ints as long as time's willing …"

Raromere's features were now famished by anxiety.

"Take this also; you will need a trustworthy gauntlet for a sure grip. A sword will be found in darker times, I'm afraid."

His once hardened eyes gave light to a small smile: small in appeal, but greatly warming at heart.

Flicking her neck, scales flowed like a wave down Syocer's back as she stationed and flexed her muscles; the flakes now made an aerodynamic jump into place. Airsing shifted the gauntlets, fastening them onto his arms as he gripped the map.

"Thank you, sir," he replied with a short bow.

He tried not to make it curt, but Syocer cut in as she heard the sound of a shrill horn.

No, thank you, Rider. You have given us more hope than you know.

†

The moon climbed quickly upon the prospect as he pulled his horse's cloth-covered face into the outside air. Thankful for the relief, he lowered his eyes toward a city of the mountainous regions around them; he was now inset in the matter called "off course", acknowledging his certainty in the fact that he was lost. He carefully uncovered the animal's eyes as he whipped the cloth through the fresh air.

Regardless of his position, he settled down on the rocky pathway with his horse, as he was too exhausted to continue the descent. His head gingerly hit the rock wall behind him as he lifted his arms to wring out his sodden garments, laying the shirt across his knees.

The horse roamed where it pleased until it found a not-too-far-off patch of dew flowers. Aware of his horse's find, Xavier half-asleep realized that those flowers only grew in the Dwarven country, which was halfway across the world, as far as he was concerned.

§

Syocer's scales felt blunt, but steadier under his gauntlets.

Airsing peered back into the darkness of the mountains, taking with him a picture of the ints clad in armor. The latter concept was now maximized in clarity, as the depiction of their souls was laid bare before his eyes, though some fluctuated in visibility. There were hundreds of knaves with spears and rough daggers marching for the gate of Alrisen.

"Syocer, we need to help them."

Rider, we would not be of any help if we stayed. More are counting on us than you know.

Airsing paused, searching for an outlet; he never found anything but a question: "Why couldn't I see the shadow the first time?"

Rarely a few can, even when they fight. You are taking on the perspective of a rider. You can see things not clear to your eyes alone; now, you can truly see the difference in realities.

"How are they going to fight them, then?"

They can see their armor, though not their soul.

His eyes followed his gauntlets as he moved his hands toward Syocer's forewings, pausing, though not enjoying the silence for that fleeting moment.

"Syocer, who's Zayin?"

He's a fighter who has a dose of wisdom beyond any, humble as he is. He has seen many pains of this war, though he is young yet.

She smiled, *You are curious for an Arqyn.*

"Arqyn ..."

This is who you are. You are the last of your kind. The characteristics of the Arqyn are many. They were ambitious workers who were very versatile in skill. They were called...to be an Arqyn is more of a calling, but blood is still vital to their race.

Syocer allowed her wings to rest on the wind as she glided into a valley, which flattened into a plain; the contour of a jagged rock seemed to block the view of what lay behind it.

†

Xavier awoke to a startling sound: clopping upon the ground, which turned out to be his horse trotting down the track to the city. As Xavier tried to stop it, pulling his shirt over his head and grasping his garment, he found himself running straight into an awe-filled mass of people as he pulled his, now dry, cloak up over his still int-like hair, looking onward toward a strange sight.

§

Syocer's wings broke the air as she landed soundly on the dirt.

Airsing found his footing on the rocky pathway, jumping from Syocer's back yet again. He looked up to see her image gleaming in his view as he shook his head; flight was still so new and invigorating to his nerves. Many stared, but he was used to the eyes, as he had felt in King Raromere's presence.

Syocer?

Airsing felt her probing mind search the crowd.

Her eyes were fixed on one who moved with a quick air, was cloaked in black, and possessed a red sword. Her muscles flexed and tried the earth as she sought Airsing.

Leave now. We need to run quickly.

She growled slightly as she swerved, talons scraping up the rocks and rubble lingering on her once stationary claws.

The on-lookers were now muddled into a hushed group, as they were taken aback by the portrayal of strength in Syocer's outstretched silhouette against the drowning sun.

Airsing held on with all his might, noticing his fingers quickly slipping from her forewings as Syocer caught herself clasping a mountain peak in her claws. Guarding his frame with her wings as she resurfaced her adrenaline, she scaled agilely into a slight catch in the mountain.

Airsing, they're looking for you...to kill you.

6

Xavier

You are the last rider ... Syocer growled in his face, displaying her righteous anger.

His hand felt the ground as he stabled himself, caringly pushing her wings from view with his other.

You are the key to the prophecy. You are the only weapon that can conquer the armies dwelt in evil.

Syocer directed her gaze into the air as her claws played the rocky ground.

He wanted to kill you. You have to use your senses. Didn't you notice his red blade?

Her wings flickered toward his brow, her own head tilted as to point to his use of intellect.

"Wait. A prophecy?"

Airsing watched Syocer's nostrils flare out in smoke.

...A prophecy that contains the beginning of these evil times...There are two prophecies: one fake, one true.

She sheathed her wings, and then drew her talons silently across the ground as she redirected her focus toward Airsing.

...One wielded for your hand, the other for your foe's. The Arqyn, Elves, Dwarves, Rav, Shilen, and one other (now dead to this realm) forged the first. No one knows what happened to it; all that remains are the stories of its once true existence.

When the dark lord, for a short time, came to power, the second was forged under the name of his companions: Xav, Syfrin, and int. A few creatures from different realms formed this pact also, though they've disappeared to this world once more.

This force outnumbered many armies, and every one on the earth was found without courage...all except for the dragon riders, who fought with a victor's bravery that seemed to make evil cringe as their swords were plunged deeply through their hearts.

Her eyes blazed in a sudden fury as she continued:

The dark lord, Arkt, led his troop into battle once again. He was killed, some say; some say he's going to rise to even a darker height when the rider comes to challenge him. Regardless of this suspicion, he took every rider and dragon's life force by manipulating the rider's soul...torturing it to the point of death...but that is all a myth to the minds of these watered-down races.

Syocer reflected as to not leave out anything.

The first prophecy reveals a time of peace, seemingly, before the war, as one Arqyn makes his destiny known.

We have a task and we must complete it, or with us the light will be extinguished...from everlasting to everlasting, or so the story goes ...

Airsing crouched by Syocer's slender foreleg as he smoothed the map upon the ground with stones.

"I say we let night fall on the valley before we make our journey into the village…Who was the int with the red sword?"

He glanced up, one arm now outstretched to keep his balance.

I can't reach his name, although...something seems different about his allegiance. His countenance seems like it wants to be found...I don't know, but I can't penetrate him...There are some things left locked ...

Airsing grew more understanding to Syocer's careful words as her attitude imbued his mind.

The moon climbed the mountains, scattering light across the stars, as Syocer's wings drew almost silently through the air.

His home is straight, there, right by the tree.

Syocer's eyes now reflected the white specks peppering the sky, as they both peered between a crack in the stonewall.

You keep hidden.

Airsing lingered a moment in her thoughts, which were already searching his mind.

Don't worry...you'll know if I'm traced...and I'll know if you're in trouble of the int's blade.

She confidently looked upon her rider as she soared into the sky, Airsing climbing the stones on the remaining skeletons of ivy.

Clank…clank…shhhk…to a halt.

Airsing's grip faltered only too quickly under the moon's glare. He regained his posture as he shrank into the shadows; the soldier now raced from the road, not making any motion of acknowledging anything but a stone's echo scrambling over the edge of the wall.

Turning his head quickly from the right, then to the left, Airsing slid his legs over the ivy-ridden stones and warily ran across the trying sound of his steps. He found the ledge as he gripped the top steadier with his palms; he started to descend as another soldier ran upon the scene.

He jumped onto the earth, caught by his hand, as he whipped the shadow of his hair from sight.

Airsing swiftly drew across Zayin's cottage as he caught a glimpse of movement.

A sword would be great right now, his thoughts echoed as if they were entreating the leaves of the trees to rustle.

A shadow flickered and quickly faltered under the revealing moonlight as a red tint caught his glare.

Shoot....

Run! Quickly ...

Syocer's eyes reentered his remembrance as Airsing cut through the foliage, letting his eyes race past the slits of darkening shade that broke through the silhouettes of trees.

He shot across the grass, never crossing the path until he came upon a Sycamore tree, ironically setting itself up as the gateway between dark and light.

Airsing rapidly climbed up the smooth bark as he jumped across the dead, hollow branches that were cracking as he went.

His breathing steadied as he fell into an opening; what once pervaded his view as a shadow was now replaced by a young man holding a clean blade, glistening upon his shoulder, and a sac, equipped to his knowledge. He motioned for silence as he grasped Airsing's shirt and yanked it taut. Airsing glanced down at the steady hand tearing at his garment; there was no time for him to think as he felt the scathing wind scar his brow.

Xavier looked down; his hands regressed eerily into the background of his gaze, escaping his visible Shilen likeness. He was fading into the woodwork, now noticing his blackening hair guarding his unmistakably red eyes.

Xavier looked up and, latching his horse to a tree, began the ascent. As his Shilen blood began to boil back into him, he felt a jolting recoil as a strange attitude infused his being.

7

Blade's End

Airsing flew into the air as the young man's grip released. The red sword was pale underneath the moon's glare as it dashed against the metal alacrity. The elf glowered at Xavier, who lowered his blade.

Xavier had an air of being sincerely stunned, more by his own ends than the parry. He felt the int-like attitude creep up on his mind as he tried to brush it away, eyes luminous in red shards. He lowered his blade as he watched the warrior confide in his thoughts, pacing the floor like a lion ready to pounce.

"Airsing ..." the voice was strong, holding an air of confidence about it.

Airsing's head nodded up at the sound of his name, now noticing that the elf's hand was still on his hilt.

Glancing at Xavier and then at the young man, Airsing adjusted his back against the wall.

Airsing's eyes now strayed to the figure by the window again; Xavier's blade was held toward the elf.

Xavier felt that he had to get rid of his weapon if he was going to purge himself of his phantom.

"Here ..." his voice succumbed to the conditions, his lips dry and parched; Xavier's red sword clashed with the ground.

"I hate the thing anyways ..."

Xavier's outstretched hand shook, as his eyes grew perplexedly aware, drawing it back into the shadows.

The elf, who-Airsing had now pieced together from the little evidence in the moonlight-was Zayin, admired the int's stance as Xavier pushed back his hood, revealing his red eyes. Xavier now rubbed his wrist as he humbly glimpsed in Zayin's direction, eyes illuminated in what seemed like crimson anguish.

"Where do your loyalties lie? If not with us, with our enemies?"

The moon strangely outlined the room, as Xavier stood upright under his critic's eye.

"I ..." Xavier's voice rang as weathered as his features, trying to find an answer.

The very vagary that he was still standing was enough to flummox his thoughts.

"Airsing, he tried to kill you. What's your will?"

Choose wisely, Rider. Destinies tampered with become a great wrinkle.

"It'll have to be his own choice. He has to master what's been tied to him."

Airsing was now straightening himself against the woodwork as he looked eye to eye with Xavier, not understanding the full gravity of his statement.

The elf smiled out of admiration, it seemed, "Your decision."

"I want to…help ..."

Xavier reflected on how strange that would sound to them as his eyes dashed to the floor, wincing slightly at his statement.

"Right now ..."

Zayin's hard glance gave Xavier the whole story.

"…I say your sword will be of that."

As Zayin took the blade, he stared mercilessly into Xavier's eyes; he believed Xavier was just posing as good, as many ints do.

Xavier shook his head as he looked down toward the floor once more. He swallowed in an effort to find his last words, but nothing ever came.

Xavier climbed down, pausing to notice how the dead limbs fell so freely after his steps. He mounted the confused animal and rode off into the aching silence.

"Your dragon's judgment was wise," Zayin started, as he swung his sac over his shoulder.

"How do you know of her?"

"Forthcomings. Signs. News of a dragon spreads like wildfire in these parts...That word isn't necessarily the ordinary subject one seems to find in everyday company...Let's see...you have been sent to me from King Raromere...I sense he told you to find me here ..." he drew from Airsing's eyes as he whipped his sword eagerly through the air.

"See this blade? It was made for a purpose. I forged it to fight."

His eyes caught Airsing's once again.

"You have to live up to your Name; you were meant for a sole purpose, Lumos...Am I right?"

His eyes flickered as Airsing's own eyes likened to his Name.

Zayin was now standing, holding out a match to, what seemed like, a finely prepared hearth of wood. The small stick, now consumed in bright gingers, fell slowly to the timber it was destined to fall upon. The fire ignited brightly into Airsing's cold features, brilliantly outlining Zayin's frame for a moment as he started back upon his rhetoric:

"If you succeed, hope. If you falter, never again will someone have that chance."

Zayin leaned back as he stationed his sword upon his other shoulder, enjoying the fleeting silence.

†

Xavier halted a second to look back on the misfortune into which he fell.

His eyes fermented into a sudden red, as a white spark shot up into the air. His horse bucked and fell forward into a gallop, taken aback by the sudden jolt. Xavier's hood fell instantly from his brow as he tried to control the stride of the bucking animal, though no amount of steering or consolation would impart a solution.

§

As the calm illustration of flitting flames fell from his gaze, Airsing's eyes filled with images of ints and Syfrin clustered outside of a familiar gate, which was all too tried to Airsing's short-term, yet curious thoughts.

Airsing!

Syocer's wings flushed his face.

Come on.

Her tail fled the aperture as Airsing leapt upon the sill of his jump. He peered about, glancing around the now consuming darkness as he motioned for Zayin's already cognizant leave; still no Syocer as Airsing looked about, sensing something so close to him, he could feel it.

The next thing he knew, he had taken a step out of an involuntary motion and was clinging to her scales; his gauntlets found one of her back wings as she started to flip through the air, allowing him to flail onto her back.

Good, you've done better this time.

What was that?

You know all too well...They're hunting you ...

Airsing didn't probe any further as he focused beneath Syocer's dangling talons; Zayin's faint form was added to the bleak circumstances, now fully under the moon's evident eyes.

Ints.

Airsing's hair shaded his brow as he looked back to see the gates of the city under siege.

I feel like we've done more harm than help, Syocer ...

You'll know the ending soon enough, Rider...We'll turn by the river, and after that, he's on his own way to Shyter.

The sky faded into the blemished red as the dim stars disappeared one by one. A piece of the sun was wedged carefully in-between two violet clouds, holding the ball of light within their hands.

The mountains by Shyter seemed tall and snow peaked at first glance, but when Syocer landed on the mountain, flowers with white leaves covered the terrain.

Arimeth flowers.

Airsing took in the unfamiliar sight with pleasure as his thoughts lingered on his exhale.

Airsing, urgency filled Syocer's voice as her thoughts silently reverberated his own.

He found a flitting reflection running through her eyes as he glimpsed backward, hearing a thump of horse hooves softening until they climbed the whole of the mountain pathway, halting under the tavern.

†

Xavier made his way through the forest, where he lodged under a small favor he could afford: a tree. His horse was sorely tired and hoped for a good rest as it searched the path for milkweed, laying itself down.

Xavier looked back, aware of the path they had escaped. He was now beginning to feel the toll on his body as his features were chastened sore by the journey's sudden expectations. His malnourished frame took notice of his surroundings, morose as they were, but faltered under exhaustion.

8

Zayin The Warrior

"I'm afraid we've gotten off without a proper introduction; my name's Zayin, as you probably know. I never thought that I would really get to see this spectacle…It's truly an honor, Rider."

He held out his hand as he dismounted, acknowledging his horse's fleeting mane flowing rapidly away from his position.

Airsing gave a strong handshake as Zayin admired the meekness.

"Thanks for your sword back there."

"Right," Zayin brushed the comment aside as he became very much disappointed at the subject.

Then he stepped into the daylight, withheld from the cave's shade, for the first time, and Airsing saw the confident warrior as he was. Young, definitive features, brown hair, and blue eyes; with feathery strands of hair and jeweled, black pupils: he was of the perfect Elven make. A bit taller than Airsing, he bowed as he trudged through the cave.

"Better start a small fire before dark deceives the signal of the flame."

He heartily brushed Airsing with his steady palm as he picked up a few rocks, examining their jagged edges and smoothing them in his hands.

The flames groped for the air as they crackled over stories Zayin conjured into the stiffness of the cave.

"…I am of Elven blood…the Elven, you know, were thought to be brothers of the Arqyn, as you are. My story starts long ago …"

His brow furrowed as he picked up more wood to feed the illuminant fire.

"As irrelevant as it is, you probably wouldn't want to hear it."

"Doesn't look like there's much else to do."

Zayin cast the pieces of timber into the blaze as he brushed the stones gingerly in his hands, positioning himself expertly on his elbow as his chin rested on his shoulder, considering the reply.

Airsing leaned against Syocer's back as his head relaxed on her gentle motion of breathing, trying to remember the last time he was home looking at the night sky.

"Good point…All right…Let's see…where do I begin? …"

He plodded one stone in his palm several times as his head cocked up; his eyes became familiar with his story as they alighted, reflecting the flames of his past:

"My father was from the range of Rivensky. I grew up in the mountains by Key…I know that land like the back of my hand, or what it used to be…no telling what Arkt has done to it …

"My father was drafted into the army. This was a while before you were born. He said that these wars would go on for a while, but there was only one thing that would make them come to rest…and that's you...."

Airsing looked up, his hair fluctuating in the wind.

"He left after that, and I never saw any sign of him again …"

"Did you ever try to find him?"

Airsing's head tilted slightly as he balanced his arms on his knees, forgetting the reference to himself.

"Of course, thousands of times. Wouldn't you?"

"Yeah, I would …" Airsing's voice withdrew in somber disappointment as he cupped his head in his hands, looking toward the dripping ceiling.

The outer world grew into lethargic discontentment as well, letting way to nostalgic remembrance.

"I have resorted to the warrior life, more like because of my journeys…Well, some time passed as I became more familiar with this blade."

He held up the slight piece of metal as his eyes studied across it.

"It's been my aid from the beginning…I've fought in some small battles, none of which had many casualties…Then, I left Key searching for revenge. As soon as I left, I'll regret, the battle of Rivensky arose…that's where my father died…he and his dragon."

"Wait," Airsing cut in, "You were alive…and your father had a dragon?"

Airsing cast his glance across the glaring embers to the warrior once more as his muscles were awakened by the new discovery.

"Yes, I was alive," Zayin sighed a laugh.

"Of course, Elven history has a good profit. Elves live longer than the Dwarves, Rav…the Arqyn have quickly died, but nobly so…They had a greater calling than most would ever hope to receive…My father was a dragon rider, though not of the race…he had a mission…Yes, my father had a noble dragon…the one that was said to have the strength to perish the dark lord …"

I thought you said he was young.

In Elven years.

Syocer's eyes danced in the fire as her head settled gently on the ground, admiring Zayin's youthful appearance.

"I'm sorry for your loss, if it helps…I don't have any folks around, except for my grandfather …"

Zayin started, but Airsing proceeded, "Ah…it's nothing; I've been used to it…after all, never known anything different."

His eyes looked up again as he rested his head on Syocer.

"Quick, douse the fire; night falls quickly these days on impatient foes."

Airsing peered from the cave. The sun's last rays were trying to quench the pervading darkness, yet never succeeded as it fell into the black ocean.

"Well, until a crossroads, my sword is yours. I'm to repay your blade."

"No …" Zayin responded, tersely relaying his thoughts.

"…But could I be of your service until the end…death or life…I should like to see those vile creatures storm in and then be taken by surprise when you escort them to their death ..."

Zayin leaned back, head against the dank wall.

Good, we can learn to trust, but doubt is something that our habits need not be taught...Keep my sense about you, Airsing.

Syocer's breathing suppressed his invigorated nerves into sleep, as his eyes faded into a realm of no dreams.

9

Two Destinies Collide

The horse was energetic, or scared out of its wits more like, when Xavier awoke to another sunrise; beautiful or not: it was red, blood red.

His green eyes now reflected on the crimson sky.

Xavier leapt to his feet and grabbed his bow, simultaneously running to lead his horse over to the edge of the forest. Something seemed strangely difficult; the swish of the leaves provoked unseemly settling suspicion as he turned to see the sun's dim light flooding the forest. Nothing there.

He gingerly mounted his horse and quietly trotted through the trees, stopping every so often to survey the aspects of the brush and the hoof marks behind him.

§

Evy gyr, arint saratir.[6]

Airsing quickly opened his eyes, jumping spiritedly upon his feet as if evading a mirage of an arrow, and pushed back the strands of blinding hair veiling his vision.

---

[6] Literal meaning: Look alive, dragon rider.

"Relax, it's only breakfast. Isn't that bad," Zayin commented as he dropped the hunt onto the rocky terrain.

"I'll prepare the coon, and I'll save a few for …"

He glanced toward Syocer, his youthful features at a loss with curiosity.

"Oh, sorry. My fault on this one…Her name's Syocer."

Airsing brushed her wings closed as she flexed them, flickering them awake.

"For Syocer, then."

He admired her strong, yet slender appearance as she quickly hoisted her head, waving the air pockets from underneath her riveting scales.

Airsing now fastened his senses onto the outside air as he took a deep breath, which pushed him back against the chilled wall he was now poised upon.

"A cross between a Tagny Ridge and a Lumiertreer Scale Talon," Zayin said, now putting the pieces together as Airsing's focus was rerouted.

"Beautiful creatures. You're the last one...but something seems different-" and just when he was getting to his point, Syocer confidently puffed a shroud of smoke toward his face.

Ty uth zíon.

Airsing laughed as Zayin battled the smoke.

"She says: you're good."

With his elbow poised on his knee, Airsing readily ruffled his feet into his work boots.

Evey?[7] he asked with an inquiring look, holding up a ferret.

Nyr[8]*…I do my own hunting.*

With her word, Syocer started for breakfast.

Furn sidra.[9]

Airsing stood for a while until his feet settled him by a rock, his tailbone aching as he sat rigidly awaiting the good rest to start relieving his muscles of the lassitude so loosely bound to him now.

"Where should our tracks lead us?"

"The ints have followed me everywhere until here, as far as I can see…I say we move toward the bridge of Lamedh."

---

[7] Literal meaning: Want?

[8] Literal meaning: No.

[9] Literal meaning: Keep hidden.

He bit into a crisp apple he had thrown into his sac, admiring the coarse sound.

"Syocer's back."

Airsing's head lifted as she swooped into the window of their view, his hair flying away from his eyes as he smiled to see her features aglow.

"She's quick in flight. I'd like to see her run."

She smiled humbly as she watched the terrain, closing her bent wings; the two packed up after Zayin's stew warmed their already excited muscles.

Airsing had hardly climbed onto her scales when Syocer abruptly took off into the almost lurid blue of the sky. She stayed low to the ground, ducking and averting branch and stone after branch.

Zayin raced behind, as Syocer quickly, though with an agile air, landed on the break of the forest.

The bridge of Lamedh.

Her eyes flooded over the narrow passage as her voice seemed to esteem the picture, which was woven years and years ago through the care of miniscule details that aged it less and less.

†

At a huge crack, Xavier's horse bucked into the air, sending his cloak, hood, and all tumbling from his frame. The horse rapidly started away from the noise, running as fast as it could until they came to a clearing. Xavier pulled on the horse's mane as it veered away from the track, pawing the ground unsteadily. As he looked up to focus through the misty clearing, Xavier's notice fell upon two Xav, undetected, approaching one on a horse and the other by a dragon.

§

The crack resounded leagues away as Airsing climbed from Syocer's back, sensing the river a few steps away from the ledge. Zayin came through the brush a while later, measuring the earth's footprints. He skimmed upward, smelling the full, crisp air as mist ordained his eyebrows.

The bridge was a sight from where they stood, ropes taut and wood still a glossy pine, standing resolutely against the placating background of the reflective water and bright plants.

"Syfrin, or bigger yet: Xav?"

Zayin nodded at his own question as he stroked his horse, which was panting like a dog.

Syocer, unseen and subtle.

She folded her wings as she quietly raced for the mountaintop to oversee their steps.

"Airsing, the people in this place are from the race of the ranger. Keep your sense, and …"

Zayin took a sheath from under his horse's blanket.

"Try this…made for a rider."

Zayin pointed the hilt in Airsing's direction as he studied his eyes: they seemed to drink the sword into an exclusive state as they sparkled its reflection inevitably.

"Thanks."

He studied the blade as his features slightly gave way to a smile.

For a darker time, right?

He tested the metal as if he had made it himself; then, he quickly fastened the sword to his belt.

Xavier's close.

Syocer's nerves ran through his veins.

"Come on, Airsing, we can make the gate in time."

Zayin was already leading his horse toward the bridge as he glimpsed back to see Airsing's vigilant ears warily reaching to uncover a trace of an unknown sound, echoing about the drums in his head.

"Wait."

Zayin turned from his horse with the rope still in his hand, the wind muffling every sound but one.

Leaves cracking.

10

Ablaze

"Ah!"

Xavier's arrows cut straight into Airsing's view. He evaded the projectiles, discovering the ground with his palms, as he looked back up to Xavier's attention that was focused in back of him.

Airsing!

Airsing's awareness faded for an instant to come back into view of a Xav pierced through the chest by Xavier's arrow.

Xavier's breathing was steady as he quickly searched the group for the other enemy. He stood, polishing his shot readily into the nock for his last mark. Before Xavier could aim, Zayin's sword pierced the next Xav through the chest, falling by his feet.

As Zayin motioned to Xavier with his eyes, his expression was one of curiosity.

Xavier quickly jumped from his perch, above Airsing, and yanked the arrow from his target.

"Only have so many …" Xavier explained as he cleaned it quickly upon the knave's disintegrating shirt, quivering both bow and arrow; he now held out his hand, which Airsing took almost without hesitation.

Airsing smiled slightly as he admired the shot. He sheathed his blade upon seeing Xavier's bow jutting out from his quiver.

Xavier reached for something obscure from Airsing's view.

"I haven't come to seek your defiance. I have something you might want to see."

His eyes irresolutely danced from Zayin to Airsing, meeting them in their astonishment.

Zayin's shoulders shrugged; his eyes were now wide with wonder.

"I have something you need to see, but not here …"

Reticently, he put the cloth back into his windswept pocket, reserving his thoughts for a safer course.

Syocer?

If you knew, you will find I'm always with you.

We can't go into a ranger city with an int.

His visibility relies solely on his loyalty. He will be visible if he is not loyal to Nyros…If he is visible, he will be seen as what he is…Zayin sees him as the interface Xavier perceives himself to be.

Xavier?

Yes, his name …

"We'll tread under the bridge. It's getting darker, and the gate will probably be shut."

"I know I'm asking more than I deserve…I'm sorry for lunging at you the first time, if sorry could cover such an act…It's kind of hard to differentiate between the int and the Shilen when you're first engulfed in everything but your own life…I'm finally getting to separate the two…I realize that my life has been forever scarred by both meeting, though."

These words were followed by Xavier's silence, his breath now submitting to the hardening heartbeat inside of his chest.

Airsing said nothing, but went back to Xavier as he steadied a friendly grasp on his shoulder, which was accompanied by a respectful smile; Airsing's dark strands of hair crept into his eyes as he looked back toward Zayin.

"Friend or unfortunate acquaintance?" the gatekeeper yelled from his watch.

"Elven ally. Zayin of Key, son of a rider deceased."

"Welcome Zayin, ally of the ranger."

The gate quietly opened as Xavier's eyes grew wary again, searching each soul to see if he could find the reflecting enemy of himself in their eyes. As he looked back to Airsing, his own eyes were still the sound influence of friendship and courage.

Zayin felt the ground with his boot, retracing his many steps as a young boy in this rugged place.

"This way," Zayin began as he whispered how he came into ownership of the cottage by his father's relocating for war.

Zayin tied his horse, holding out his hand for Xavier's roped reins; Xavier carefully rejected Zayin's courtesy, nodding as he tightened the rope to the same post.

The room was dark before Zayin lit a single flame, cupping it in his hands. Xavier then closed the door with an almost inaudible crack of the wooden panels as if he was used to being as invisible.

"I guess you'd expect this, but I'm still not fully acclimated to trusting you …" Zayin's blade flashed as he leaned casually back upon the wall.

The flame flickered as Xavier took the cloth into his scarred hands, clutching it as he positioned his elbows on his knees.

"Good to meet you too …" Xavier's eyes held a certain melancholic color about them now as he bowed his head to his focus.

"But, true…I understand more than you know…."

They exchanged introductions curtly as the silence lengthened into a certain expectation, watching Xavier's hands, as their scarred appearance seemed to be holding a very promising sight.

His face was immersed in awe-filled wonder as he kept the cloth in the light.

The material appeared void until he burned a side; as Xavier anticipated his next move to be successful, he set the whole cloth ablaze.

The darkness grew in the room until one spark jumped.

Crack!

11

All In A Cloth

The room illuminated in flickers of fire as the remnants of light filled the corners and air with, what seemed like, markings and names of regions: a map, but something else invigorated the very wooden structure in which it was now entrapped. A legend, written, exploded into sparks. The flames moved rapidly around the small room, evading the three, as the sparks now shed light and wind through their frames.

"These have been hidden in the mountains for centuries ..."

"How did you-?"

"I don't know...the map of the four winds and the true prophecy written in fire...I can't believe it! I've heard of it in stories, but nothing like this!"

Xavier followed a stationary flame with his fingers as he reflected on the conversation.

"Here, the Xav are stationing at Rivensky."

As he pointed, the flame, representing the region, grew larger in detail.

"Then, there was something about Sant Key...possibly a passage to another conquering ground ..."

He began searching through the flames as he stood, redirecting his focus off of the lights just above his white-tipped hair.

And as he found a familiar spark, he uttered, "Here…Then, they are planning to siege the range of Arqdrak and make it their dwelling. They'll move quickly, but this goes without saying.

"All this while, the Syfrin are mustering an army at Nyros, a subtle approach to some sort of reinforcement. And that's all I've got...The task?"

He shrugged his broad, yet slender shoulders.

"Gather as many soldiers on your side as possible, and stop the Xav from taking the Shilen hold as well as the Elven. Keep in mind that they might take Sant Key into the passage of Thela if their plan fails."

Zayin was watching Xavier speak; he no longer appeared as an int with red eyes and jet-black hair; his features were alive with silvering hair and green eyes reflecting the true internal, the key, of his soul.

Airsing wandered around the room, his shadow dancing across the now illuminated floor, as he listened intently to the details being laid bare before him.

"I say the first place we try is the city of the Rav in Terranith. Shoot! And time …"

Airsing's feet led him to the prophecy as he halted involuntarily before the sparks.

"I've no clue about the time, but I'd venture to guess eleven days till they pass Rivensky…then the rest is up to them. I would think that large of an army would take about seventeen days until they decide they're ready to take the field…They're not a small force to reckon with, I'll tell you that much …"

Xavier's eyes lit as if something had been overlooked, "I should mention…they have watch on the skies from Nyros to the four winds. They see every bird, every leaf. You don't want to take a chance with your dragon."

Airsing heard faintly the sound of his voice as he concentrated on the prophecy:

As timely shadow makes age Dark
And Nyros breaks its evil grip,
As the plot of Rivensky remains in scar,
A time. A woe
Will pass as a slow,
Unceasing burden.
To kill a sword is given

One hope.
Repels a looming despair
One race of rider
To embrace the true destiny
In motion.
One creature to guide the steps of
A warrior.
If the One shall not pass the
Merciless gate,
The End of all things is Near.

One warrior and creature with companions from unexpected places.

Airsing peered into the words; as lights flashed into his eyes, a phrase materialized as he blew the flames from before his sight:

Lumos, tir a treer arint saratir.

His mind flashed back to the first time he saw Syocer.

"If the One shall not pass the Merciless gate, the End of all things is Near."

He kept his eyes on the smoke that remained, his eyes dwindling on the emblazoned phrase.

Xavier stared into his features that were, at this point, unmoving.

"You all right?"

He cocked his head, as Airsing didn't respond, obviously deep in thought. Flames were moving, flickering through his eyes.

Seven days.

"We have seven days."

"How did you-?"

"Syocer."

"Who's-?"

"The dragon."

Zayin got a kick out of knowing something he didn't for the past few minutes.

12

Seven

Xavier gathered the flames, as the room grew suddenly dark.

"We have to leave, or we'll never make it in time. We need the speed of horses."

Zayin's horse moved quickly as the rough terrain was steady underneath its hooves, leaving the calm demeanor of the village exposed to a waning, yet early dusk.

Syocer, return to land. It's not safe in the air.

Haven't I told you: I'm always with you...Remember to use my senses...tell Xavier not to be alarmed.

"Xavier, this is Syocer," Airsing said as he smiled, Syocer's entrance seeming sound and agile as Xavier's eyes brightened at the sight.

"Amazing."

Airsing turned and stroked Syocer's snout as her eyes reflected the clear, silvering skies. They looked toward the narrowing pathway before them, laden with leaves and brush as it stretched into the horizon.

Airsing took a moment to watch the place they were deserting, but Syocer diverted his eyes to look forward as she whipped him upon her back with her tail.

Syocer's movement felt much like a horse's, except lighter and faster, the ground feeling similar to air as the journey proved long into the night.

"The plateau of Kaph" looked strangely far from their position. The moon was reaching for its place as the stars recollected their light. Their steps were parched from the whites and blues now lingering before them; the land was red and rocky, withstanding the valley's eroding view. Mountains loomed on the horizon, poised hopefully on the last glimpse of sun as the travelers descended toward their goal. With the stars gracing the sight, the scene appeared surreally tranquil, but to no one's attention.

Zayin started, "We'll keep by the river of Heth tonight. We have no time to stop until we are from the plain of Aleph."

Xavier's stories became of good help to pass the time of the lengthening journey: "Before I became an int, captured by the Syfrin, I was full blood Shilen."

"I'm still astounded that you chose Shilen…Finding the light, few ever come across it," Zayin's words faded as they threw their audibility upon a rushing stream.

Syocer surveyed the land, gliding over the body of water.

"What are you skilled with?" Zayin asked.

"The sword, mostly; some say you can give me a bow and I'll do just as well."

Xavier smiled, his silver hair catching glimpses of his deepening green eyes. These two kept conversing in the backdrop as Airsing kept probing through the forest before them.

"In all my ages, I've never seen an int turn ways. Remarkable. The creatures never smile, never laugh…except for someone's pain; though never really…never care for anything other than their self-survival…You've made a great journey. Let's hope out of ints you'll stay," his voice grew solemn, though brushed with a splash of jest as it was; he cast his attention through the deepening woods.

Xavier quickly brushed the shadowing past from his mind as his voice wavered for an instant, "I'm never going back to the dark days of wretched wandering, listless joy, and hopelessness for the day ahead …

"Never again will I be allied with the dark wretches who take innocent blood, fill their hearts with uncertainty and shakable objects of scorn…They're senseless, faithless, heartless, and ruthless…never again."

His brow furrowed as he took a deep breath, remembering his father.

His soul is strong, Airsing…He is truly remarkable…though he is not yet aware of the power he wields …

Airsing looked backward, questioning Syocer's thoughts. The prospect becoming clear, Xavier's tightening grip clutched his bow as his horse started to buck backward.

"Watch your step, something is vigilant in these woods."

Airsing, evy aelf![10]

He looked up to see legions of tiny lights crashing to the ground, freezing, and then shooting through the air with an energy that sent the company recoiling into a phase of painful fluctuations. The snowy particles were now a barrage of dust, veiling to their view.

Zayin pulled Xavier up as he yelled, "Head south! They're trying to cut us off!"

"Go…go!" Xavier urged as they almost stalled at the sight.

Airsing flattened himself against Syocer's scales as she ran through the woods, keeping a solid pace for Xavier and Zayin's horses; the lights were now numerous, creating a picture that dared to crash through the windows made by the trees outlining the sight. Their eyes flipped through the scene as the source of these lights was now more veiled from their speculations than ever before.

Airsing's body felt Syocer's every muscle tense and relax as her slender body sniped through the forest.

Syocer, whatever you do, don't jarny[11].

Airsing glanced back for one moment to see the horses riding on her tail, explosions closing in on them until one crashed into Syocer, sending her scales rippling away from the burning sensation; Airsing flew into the air as he felt heat surge through his whole body.

Syocer's wings propelled forward, jerking Airsing from the light's explosion in one sinuous action.

Xavier yelled something, but Airsing couldn't make it out; his muscles were failing his will to hold on as they immobilized

---

[10] Literal meaning is uncertain, though may be used in this simplified context as: cast your gaze toward heaven!

[11] Literal meaning: Fly.

stiffly, which Syocer sensed as her clear wings enveloped his legs in the now reflective barriers around him.

The moment froze, as Syocer's eyes began to sense an unhindered projectile sneaking through the forest. Airsing's form was now hunkering over Syocer's back as she leered toward the periodically lightening darkness, only to come in contact with the reality: an arrow drew through the shroud, predestined for Airsing's heart.

The unconscious side of Syocer's thoughts had begun to accept the pain as her own, giving relief to Airsing's already waning liveliness. Abruptly, she lifted one appendage, sensing the point of the arrowhead acutely penetrating her mind as it did the same to her wing.

Airsing breathed sharply as the invigorating sensation fell from his heart into Syocer's scathed nerves; she growled slightly as the scene now anticipated a greater expectation, speeding up into the regular motion as it appeared (though blurred to Airsing's sight).

Then, Xavier's words came to Syocer's ears, as her eyes dashed behind her in fury.

"Syfrin."

Xavier's bow, glaring his anger, was raised into the air, as Zayin's sword kept a steady conviction in his grasp; the cold became more palpable as hazes of gray smoke rose from the destructing fireworks, mingling with the white clouds forming from their breath.

Airsing's eyes narrowed in an effort to see as he made out the Syfrin thirstily drinking in the sight of his heart; the whole scene slowed to a halt before their very eyes, as the gelid lights flashed around them.

13

A Foe Of A Friend

The Syfrin peered from the cloaked shadows that concealed his true form, his attention catching Xavier's familiar posture.

"Prepare to die, Duma."

Xavier's eyes, now blazed in muddy crimson, reddened in rage, recalling his int days.

"Xavier?"

A small, grimaced laugh gave way to the Syfrin's pride, "To give up your rank is foolish, son. You are on a death march."

The Syfrin's skull-face penetrated the air, cringing with the evil luminosity of a smile.

Xavier's hand was readily on his bow.

"Shull I take the first shaut, master Duma?" Xavier's features were now outlined with the falling lights as his intish accent crept upon him, remembering the inundating changes of his past:

Xavier's small hand clinched a wooden sword and waved it playfully in front of Duma's face. Of course, this was when Duma was a boy by the name of Yakr with brown hair. He knew him as a friend then.

"You couldn't fire the first arrow...You've changed, Ÿr ..." Duma played on his memories.

Xavier's hand wavered, but it was now steadied as he keenly pronounced his angling arrow into the nock of his bow, casting a shadow across his indecision.

Zayin couldn't watch anymore as he stepped his horse into a full speed run. Syocer growled in a long puff of smoke to divert the Syfrin's attention as he looked back in time to see Zayin's sword driving through his heart, his own parried from sight.

"That was always your weak point, Yakr...couldn't hold a parry ..."

Xavier's green eyes hardened in anguish as he aimed two arrows in the place of the other Syfrin, his Shilen likeness appearing more evident in just the few moments he stood so confidently.

Duma smiled as he fell to the ground, "You are dead, Shilen."

The Syfrin's cloak flooded with dust, flying from the ashes that were trailing from the smoke.

The two others lunged for Zayin, but found that Xavier's arrows were justly aimed as the projectiles hit the two squarely in their foreheads.

"Syfrin turn to ash when they die, as do the Xav...but you already know that ..." he said this out of the simple want to change the subject; he couldn't think of anything else to say at the moment.

Xavier sighed slightly as he looked away from the disintegrating vestiges, eyes blinking incessantly as if to blink away a terrible memory from his mind.

"He was Duma, of the minor Syfrin. He always hated me because in duels, he never caught my blade."

Putting his bow away, Xavier watched Syocer's wandering eyes; she searched his throughout as she saw that they were greener than before.

"Thanks Zayin, wow...not used to having someone back me up...kinda nice."

He smiled faintly as Zayin hit him on the back in acknowledgment.

Seemingly at the end of his thoughts, Zayin mumbled, "...though cocky as you are ... "

At this, Xavier smiled even brighter, though his eyes were still fraught with pain.

"What's taken Airsing?" Zayin inquired, uncertain of the blazing lights.

"A light, a bludger of fire. Syocer kept him holding on, though...."

Airsing's face was covered with soot, and his eyes grew as white as the newborn sky, now drawing nearer to blue when acclimated with the sun's rays. Never had a sky been so speculative, awaiting the forming clouds to cover the atmosphere.

Airsing, focus on me...Keep your eyes opened and stay lucid for a little longer ...

Syocer's voice was the only thing that was clear; she tried to search for his thoughts as he wavered between conscious and unconscious waves of pain.

Airsing tried to find something, at most something, to hold onto as his mind fluctuated between surreal apparitions and reality.

Airsing, hold on to me.

The day rose as they finally retreated into the valley, resting on account of the evening's events.

Xavier watched as Zayin tried to sturdy Airsing's steps, faltering on the first few.

"Nasty light. I've seen many of those...taken good warriors. Sit here, Airsing."

Xavier looked around the valley for something that was seemingly out of his reach as his cracked mouth gave way to his probing mind, "Zayin, you know what Cur root[12] looks like?"

"Yeah...hold on a sec'...those are the ones with the thorny leaves and the smooth, internal glasophagus[13], right?"

Zayin's eyes met Syocer's, which were twinkling at his old, Elven lingual.

"You had a valiant rescue." Zayin now gazed into the white sky of morning as he smiled at his sentence.

Xavier came up the valley in a lively spirit as if he was reveling in the great success of finding his prey.

---

[12] A Rav herb characterized by some sort of healing background.

[13] A glasophagus was an Elven word, ancient for "sac", or in the cases of Cur root: the inner sac with distinguishable dew or herb resin inset in the folds.

"Cur root...I can fix these and they'll cool his body down. In the mean time, we need some breakfast and wood."

Xavier dribbled the few pieces of timber he had retrieved for the elixir onto the ground as he now peeled and shaved the root, tearing it into the broth and stirring the liquid as he went.

"I'll gather the rest and maybe find some good game...."

Zayin kept his sword as he ventured into the woods, which offset the stark colors of the valley.

The stew smelled potent to Airsing's senses as he became aware of the cloudy outlines of the fire; he struggled to discern even the easiest of forms.

Xavier looked up to witness how the shock was advancing. Airsing's eyes grew whiter until he didn't even possess a pupil left by which to see. Xavier quickly mixed the herb and poured it into a cask. He handed it to Airsing, who could barely make out the outline of the container.

"Airsing, take this ..."

Xavier took Airsing's hand and placed it around the cask as he wiped a lash from view.

Airsing ... Syocer guided his mind as it settled down upon the liquid in the cask.

His eyes developed into an evidently transparent blue as he downed the liquid.

"Thanks Xavier, I've never seen such an explosion…almost isolated my senses."

Xavier nodded in approval as he smiled, satisfied at his expertly means.

Airsing felt an earnest pain run from his chest, familiar to him in the valley. His eyes were now perusing Syocer's.

"Xavier, is there any honey comb in this valley? Syocer's been caught by an arrow head."

Xavier leapt upon his sore feet, as did Airsing, to search for a comb.

You, my friend...I could have never made it without you.

Airsing lowered his head into her eyes as his eyebrows were now raised in an expressive "thanks". Syocer hoisted her snout as she brushed his hair with the wind of her nostrils.

We're a team. If one goes, the other also.

Zayin appeared from the brush as he watched his new ally climb his way to a novel point of interest. Xavier had found a beehive in which he quickly flushed out the bees in a skillful thrust as he gathered the comb, giving the remains to Airsing.

"You're better than a bear, Xavier ..." Zayin commented as he set his sac down upon the firewood that had spilled out of it.

"So you said you were Shilen?"

"Full blood. Most now are half." Xavier whipped his silver hair quickly from his eyes, answering Zayin's query with a sort of joking pride.

Xavier rekindled the fire, as Zayin poured more of the wood onto the ground. Seeming as if he couldn't have any more room left in his sac, he then proceeded to take out a few apples and set them one by another.

"I found the ferrets in my sac…almost forgot I'd saved them…a bit gamey, but they'll do. I got a coon in a Rav trap…that's a good find."

"And you're better than a fox…I forget how long it's been since I've had something to eat…well, besides a bit of bread to chew on…and a few horse leaves."

Xavier looked up at his horse, which was already chomping ravenously at an apple; he took out a small flint knife to another red delight, placated by the very sight of it.

They set up the fire to a better pitch, as the ferrets became the main course, Zayin skinning only two.

"One day. We have six more left," Xavier commented as Airsing got up and stiffly tried his feet again on the mottled ground.

Airsing examined Syocer's wound as Xavier watched, biting into the juicy piece of fruit. He took the arrowhead carefully from her wing and threw it to the ground as Syocer hushed a small growl.

I'm great, really. Rather have you alive than my wing.

"Nasty bite. She took a great one for you, Airsing."

Xavier rekindled the fire's dwindling light as a wind drove the sparks from the heart of the flame.

Back there...I felt that arrow driving into my nerves.

Airsing's eyes kept flooding over the gash.

Few dragon riders ever develop that sense, especially the dark ones.

Syocer growled softly as Airsing plated the wound with honey.

Sorry ...

All right. You trust me as I do you.

"Dragons are amazing creatures," Zayin stated, awakening his wonder once more.

Xavier glanced between the two.

"Since we have to wait here awhile...why does it seem like dragons are something familiar to you?" Xavier was curious, stumbling over the pieces of apple in his mouth, licking the small trail of juice from his wrist.

"My father had a dragon."

Xavier's eyes were now taken with the rocks that were exposed by the flames.

"I'm sorry ..." Xavier started, as he regretted his ever asking the question, Zayin's answer revealing the absence of his father.

Airsing held onto Syocer's scales as he found Zayin's eyes wandering into his.

Xavier twirled the apple core in his fingers, watching the fire grow with the ferrets now roasting in the smoke.

Airsing ripped off his sac cover and reached inside of it. He grabbed a ferret he had taken and gave it to Syocer.

Nyr.

You have to eat.

Not unless you do.

You're stubborn: you know that?

His eyebrows rose as he threw the animal back in the sac.

Is often thought of as strong willed, she smiled.

Go gather your ferrets. Furn sidra.

Syocer found herself upon her claws, shaking her wings freely as a few scales shattered to the ground; she ran across the earth as if it was air in her wings.

Airsing's eyes dashed to the ground with the flecks of ivory that had fallen from Syocer's wings; he cradled one scale in his hand, stroking the smooth iridescence with his eyes. He pocketed the article involuntarily and focused on the smoke now twirling away from their breakfast.

As the ferrets suited the watery broth, the stew seemed bitter, but warmed their aching bones.

Zayin took out an object made of Pidre wood[14], feeling the familiar curves and grooves.

"Is that-" Xavier marveled, as he set down his stew for a moment, only to take it back up after rubbing his dusty hands together.

"An imglö[15]? Yeah...my father's...not for travysting[16], though. It was used in the battle of Rivensky to relay messages by phoenix...."

Syocer quickly ran along the road as the frequent gusts of wind from her wings, now flailing in their faces, quelled the fire.

Airsing, quickly! she growled.

They're surrounding the valley ...

Airsing readied Zayin and Xavier as they saddled their horses, dousing the flame of their trace. Xavier kicked the logs throughout the small clearing and ran to mount his horse, as he slung his bow about his shoulders. Airsing found Syocer's wings at the last second as he propelled himself upon her back.

Syocer left the ground's stability as she cleared a trench, though not spanning her appendages. She looked back as she hesitated for a moment, eyes brightening into Airsing's, who mouthed her thoughts perfectly:

"Xavier's fallen."

---

[14] Usually from the bark of the Pidre tree, the wood is smooth and takes on characteristics similar to its unique curves and winding grain.

[15] An Elven tool used to travyst or to relay messages by smoke or fire. One useful feature about this tool is: the origin from whence the message comes can't be traced by the receiver in case of interception.

[16] A common Elven term known as: "the art of forming shapes with smoke" or sometimes "fire for sport". The art forms would usually take on a certain livelihood and try to defeat the other from advancement.

14

The Growl That Broke The Mountains

Slashing rain began to zing off Syocer's scales as slices of lightning split the sky.

Zayin trudged his way through the ominous darkness of the apprehensive measure behind him, as Syocer's vision drew in the dark atmosphere.

Xavier's fallen under...Airsing, the Syfrin ...

Without a second thought, Airsing dismounted and ran through the muddy ground as quickly as he could sprint through the current. Working against the mire, he came upon Zayin's horse straying; Airsing grabbed its reins as he was startled by a voice.

"Rider ..."

The confident hint revealed the owner of the tone as one of an unfamiliar, yet strikingly acute background.

Syocer pervaded Airsing's thoughts: *Leave.*

"Where are they?"

Airsing whipped the stinging rain from his brow as he concentrated, more intent on the sound of the voice.

"Who wants to know? ..." the tone resounded with a thunder clap.

"What is your name, boy?" the pitch grew impatient, almost daring him to take a step further into the shadows.

"You have no right to understand it …" he began, feeling his sword's hilt, "But if you don't mind, I think I'll give it to you."

Airsing's gauntlets rested on his iridescent sword, as pings of rain now shattered across the blade.

"You can call me Lumos-"

His soul seemed to flicker for an instant, the mirage merging with Syocer's being as blades of light now made up his form; a luminosity emanated into the shadows around him as the Syfrin disappeared into the sky, Syocer's voice ringing throughout his thoughts and into the atmosphere.

Lumos…saratir arint. You finish the task…finish it … her voice faded.

Syocer-

The storm quieted his thoughts.

"Syocer!"

His adrenaline pushed throughout his body as he felt swords from every angle pierce his ribs. He gripped his sodden shirt as his knees bowed to the earth; his body surrendered to the blades that were trying to find his heart, blood watering the muddy marsh.

†

"Xavier!" Zayin's voice was very welcomed in the spot in which he found himself.

"Zayin, keep quiet …"

Xavier's arrow rose as Zayin crept down onto the forest floor next to him.

"See up there?" Xavier's whisper was almost inaudible over the thrashing rain flooding the ground.

Zayin nodded, fixing his grip more steadily toward the wet, moving soil.

"Syfrin are surrounding this whole area …"

Zayin pulled his sword now silently from its sheath, wondering what two could do against the many warriors around them.

Xavier resented his next move, but something had to break the silence.

Etching three arrows in his nock, he fired, hitting all three on their mark. At the sight of the commotion, the two scurried for another cover as the Syfrin stormed to the source of the shots.

"You think we're being surrounded?" a harsh, yet wavering voice whispered through the rain.

"No, you fool! Keep going ..." another clutched his reins and led into the eye of the storm.

"Xavier-"

Xavier put up a hand to his friend's mouth, keeping his eyes fastened tautly on two Syfrin who were quietly skulking through the woods toward them. Zayin perceived their boots slashing into view as he noticed the vulnerable spots at their backs, the lightning availing the sight for a blow.

Xavier kept his eyes on the two as his arrows drew, unhampered, through the rain; upon penetrating the soft-back of the armor, Xavier climbed swiftly over the disintegrating bodies, muddled by the downpour, as Zayin followed, lingering close to the rocky sides.

"Hey you!"

Xavier quickly leapt into view of the swordsmen, allowing his poised arrows to be the main interest.

Zayin quickly took advantage of the Syfrin's shock and plunged into the mass of them, as Xavier covered him with his shots.

All lay silently disintegrating, all except for one that is. Zayin and Xavier went into hot pursuit of him.

"I'll cover his flank!" Xavier yelled as he ran up the rocks, dragging his sodden garments through the slick ground.

Zayin kept a steady mark on the Syfrin, despite the thickening rain, as Xavier and he met at the bottom, outnumbered by the surrounding army.

"Well, it sounded like a good idea ..."

Xavier pushed the oncoming spikes away from his eyes unabashedly.

"Was the only thing we could do, friend ..."

Zayin looked up at the rain, now seeming to drag them deeper into the mud.

"I only hope Airsing's well on his way now ..."

Sword held high and arrows poised, the two waited for the first blow, until a deadening growl filled their ears.

§

Airsing's blood tainted the earth, falling to the ground. He could feel his life sifting through his hands as he held on with all his might, his soul groping for life. He heard one last sound as he lay almost lifelessly in the slashing downpour.

Syocer's cry shattered the very swords around him.

Airsing's determination held him on for a while as he found himself on something very coarse, as hot as the breeze flying through his hair.

The only thing he could do was think, *Syocer*?

His body grew cold; his life rushed from his veins.

Next time ... the voice was so familiar to his thoughts, it revived him, *trust me* ...

He felt the hot, jagged ridges pierce through his rough gauntlets.

Airsing grew warm for a second as he feebly stroked Syocer's back, losing his vision into darkness as his drenched garments clung to his wounds.

He found himself in a wet stream of blood; upon looking up, he saw Syocer's nostrils flaring above everything else.

We're in a forest, her voice was holding back the anguished wear, trying to overpower the rushing rain now muffling her movements.

"Hold on...You're not gonna let go...Keep your eyes focused...Syocer?"

Her eyes kept probing for his voice to resound in her head.

"We're getting through this. We're going to make it-"

Airsing started to cough uncontrollably as he felt a trickle of blood escape his mouth, rushing his sleeve up to wipe it away from sight.

Leave, Syocer reiterated, but the tone was now frailer.

Airsing pushed Syocer to her feet as best as he could; he mustered every inch of his remaining blacksmith strength, shaking as he stood. Scrutinizing, Airsing quickly scaled the deep cuts and wounds as his eyes developed in animosity for the ones who did this.

What happened?

His focus ran over the wounds again, his shaking hands hovering over her scales.

I'll tell you later, for now we need all the strength we can get ... she sighed, growling through the sickening pain.

Airsing climbed onto Syocer's back gingerly as he cut his wounds freshly open. He inhaled sharply as Syocer's brusque movement hit the sky.

We can't fly-

I did it once; we can do it a second time.

The forest was close to Syocer's talons as her blood quickly fled from her scales, watering the canopy. The Rav were near, but Syocer's strength was fading too quickly.

Syocer ... His voice echoing through the void air, he sought for a sign of optimism in the gelid rain.

He felt her heart beat lightening as he acted in haste, saving them both.

Sucöf![17]

Syocer's speed increased, as Airsing was left in darkness, hanging by her weakening talons.

---

[17] Literal meaning is uncertain, though may be: Focus; As one; Revive.

15

Heart Of A Dragon

His strength greatly faltered when he came to, eyes clouding over as he tried to get up and find Syocer.

The hazy figures around him were speaking in a strange tongue, while all he could muster were his thoughts.

I'm with you, Airsing. Keep still. This place isn't safe.

The words swiftly ended as a sturdy hand kept him down on the ground; he lost the light and drifted into a dream.

"You failed," a calm voice rang throughout an atmosphere of uneasiness.

"Yes…sir. You must-" a soldier started, hesitating over his tongue.

"I gave you a task and the men with which to accomplish it…Why didn't you bring him to me?"

"It was dark, and the dragon was lost after she was pierced several times through the heart," again, the voice was fleeting under the mercy of the first.

"In all fairness, sir?" a sly tone entered the room, monotonously searching the disposition of the first, as he appeared almost bored at the state.

The first man acknowledged his presence.

"No dragon has ever withstood seven stabs through the heart. This is no ordinary beast of a dragon."

The cunning figure slowly skulked into view of the scarce lights now shedding clarity over his cloaked face.

"And the boy?"

"The boy was taken as dead…st-stabbed in the heart also…He was left on the ground. After a few days, his dragon will die of the loss …" the soldier's tongue was now quelled by the furtive influence:

"The young man who was stabbed through the heart is *alive*…he has escaped, my lord."

The cunning figure leered back toward the soldier in dissatisfaction.

The room seemed to glow in unrest as the man compensated for the soldier's slight of tongue, the first resolving action, "Muster the armies. Prepare for battle. Take Sant Key this time…gather men if you have to inculcate their duty into them! Seize Alrisen's stronghold and get the boy! If he escapes, we'll begin the war, and then, he will have to appear before us …"

Airsing, look alive.

His eyes slashed into the air as he wrapped his arm around Syocer's neck; she steadied his balance as he staggered upward.

I know what you took for me to live.

You also, Rider. I've seen the dream. It's real …

How could you take seven?

You took seven yourself. When a rider and dragon are one, they are stronger in will and soul.

Steps ricocheted outside the hall; the sound glanced at the two casually as if to point to their oblivious composure.

Grab your sword.

As he turned, Airsing's sight focused on a familiar face, all scarred, though smiling.

"Xavier. Never saw a warrior so alive."

Airsing sheathed the blade once readily in his hand.

"Lucky for us, we thought you were dead."

Just when he said this, Zayin climbed the pathway into the light as they acknowledged his presence.

They defended as long as they could.

"We lost you in the woods …"

They relayed their first actions and how they triumphed over a few Syfrin.

Xavier heard a faint step, one that was meant to be concealed, and at this, he took over the story, "…an army. We heard an amazingly deafening sound. It shattered the rocks and gave everything a woeful feel …"

His pupils met Airsing's as he motioned toward the hallway; his green eyes shattered in pieces of crimson. Xavier's hint gave light to Airsing's listening ears.

Brusquely, a man entered the room, his appearance turning quickly. He was tall, possessed a certain lack of courtesy, and had black hair extending from his brow as he quickly brushed his shoulders back. The tufts of hair jutted out aptly around his ears, as his expression gave way to stone, as is the trait of the Rav; his features were defined as such, but there was something different about him.

"So, this is the dragon and her rider...My name is no meaning in your tongue, so it is of no importance. If you will, come this way."

He quickly turned and ran through the passages that were winding through the structure.

"The Syfrin are heading to Rivensky?" voices quietly trailed through the lower rooms, rattling through the apertures and running upon the cobblestone walls.

"We'll have three more days to run in Arqdrak."

Syocer came around the corner into a stone room lit by a cut in the wall.

"Here are they who will help you."

The guide stepped back, holding out his hand triumphantly; his eyes turned to rocks, now lifeless as the very stones they portrayed.

"Not in bad shape after what they've taken."

He smiled wryly as he searched the dragon's features.

"Confident bravery," was taken from Syocer's scowling eyes.

"My name is Yaj. The Syfrin have a few days to get here. I ask you if you will join our side to fight against their army."

"Thank you, sir."

Syocer, we have to leave. Does he think we're this dense?

"Since we haven't had any fresh air, could we have a league of space and keep our strategy moving?"

"Wise. The guard will assist you."
"No, we'll be fine." *After all, we are enemies.*

16

Escape

The fresh air released Airsing's mind as Syocer's own flew through the clouds in the sky, free from the barred city. The atmosphere humidly interrogated their ragged clothing, as they started to wander nonchalantly about the outskirts of the fortification.

After plunging a sword effortlessly into the guard, urged on them to be their "defense", Airsing was well out of range when he and Syocer decided to run.

Zayin and Xavier ran behind as Xavier replied to their efforts, "They'll see us. We have to be more subtle than *that*!" his whisper seemed to grow in shock as his hands crouched below his now folded knees; they lied in wait for a signal of pursuit.

"We don't even have horses to outrun those fiends …"

Zayin was curious until he quickly pulled the pieces together, Xavier filling in the few that were left vague.

"He was the head of the Syfrin army. He always glared with his bad eye, the white one. He wouldn't notice me because I'm visible as a Shilen," Xavier now smiled, sharply mocking his means of explanation as he now waited for Zayin to pick up on the trails he left unmarred.

"They're now perceptible as what they want to be seen as...and that of the Rav, but where the Rav have gone: I have no idea."

His now white hair poised indefinitely into his eyes, as he made no motion to acknowledge this fact.

"Under Arkt's reins no doubt…so, they've taken Riv and turned it into a dark allure," Zayin reassured his ears.

"Where are we going?"

Syocer?

Tell him to use his father's tools.

"The phoenix."

Syocer answered Airsing's question, contemplating the flight of the bird: *There might be a chance it could make it, but it'd be slim. Remember I flew…after everything else. It's our best shot…it's all we have until we reach the end of the Rav territory.*

Zayin's imglö was emanating into a phoenix when they heard a Syfrin's horse (Their horses are notable because of their silent hooves, where only their breathing betrays their presence.) panting into the clearing.

Syocer swiftly led them into a niche, their latter part barely clearing the path behind them before:

"We've lost them."

"Your fault. *You've* failed."

Not an instant later, a blade was sheathed as the mocker's head cascaded along the forest floor.

The horse's breath drew into the woods as Airsing moved into the overhanging shade of the dark path. He emerged further into the woods as he looked toward the sky, which was veiled by the fog now quickly dissipating from sight.

"We need to find Kiren. It'll be hard...."

Airsing leered after their pursuer as he plunged deeper into the forest; his ears were tuned to even the slightest sound, making a few leaves rustling under the wind's breath into a barrage of arrows at his back.

As they followed him, the firebird returned with a burnt cloth clutched in its talons. As it descended into the hand of Zayin, so did the burnt material.

Xavier watched as it unfolded into the air, now more evident as it appeared before the fog.

The king.

We've taken the region of Alrisen. Anything else you want to give up?

Zayin threw the imglö into the canopies of the trees, watching as it exploded into sparks of burning ash, the bird disappearing in flames.

"Arkt," Xavier shot back in a wise, yet stern tone.

"Where did it come from-?"

Airsing looked toward both, eyes deciphering the possibilities.

"From Gnir, probably…I'm afraid the city of Arithmere is under siege."

Airsing, there is hope.

...And it's across the rivers of Armour and Ayint, through Guardian Mountains and into Kiren's Feather Plain; if they catch us there, we'll find an alternate route to the Fortress ...

...We have to fight him.

"Are you ready?"

"We're not going home, if that's what you think…I should shudder at the thought! You have my sword, Rider."

"And mine. No offense, but I don't think you could get through without us!" mused Zayin as he messed up Airsing's hair, Xavier laughing.

Each one of them knew that if they lingered a moment more, they would be running into a mess of Syfrin, so, naturally, they began to run through the forest, away from their pursuers, as phantoms of voices trailed through the trees and proved their efforts useful.

"There!"

"See the smoke, you idiot? Stupid int, go now!"

Xavier recalled, "Yeah, like we could've taken all those Syfrin on without Syocer's intervention?"

Airsing's mess of hair nodded up as a smile broke through his tired eyes.

To get through this, it will be harder than anyone has imagined. It will take bravery, courage, and most of all: the heart to never look back.

17

Rivers Of Armour

The rivers were white and long, as they sought a crossing. Every so often, the tide broke and crashed into their already over-soaked garments.

The scales of Syocer straightened and shook the vapor away from the gleaming glint of the sun, as the sound of the rushing river hit their ears even more rapidly; another wadi rushed upon them, turning them over like a leaf in the merciless wind.

A solid plot of land was quite welcomed to their soaking frames as they rested, more fumbling upon the island than given to rest.

Xavier's eyes raced through the waters to give his squinting muscles time to recover from the sun's glare.

Clouds now cumulated in the horizon, overshadowing the peaks of the far-off mountains.

As the moon split the sky and the last of the currents were met, even the ominous woods looked inviting after the long march across the sodden ground. The shade of the trees peppered the ground eerily as they seemed to drip through the dirt-laden path.

"...and then you place your blade as a parry attack ..." his voice galvanized the clash of swords.

"Nice."

Airsing marveled at Xavier's skills as he managed a smile, sheathing his thoughts.

"Hey, Rider…you don't think you could try that light again?"

"How'd you know about that?"

He looked from Xavier to Syocer as he cleared a log, palm quickly guarding his sword and involuntarily taking it back up again as he whipped it around in his hands.

"It reached into the sky for nine leagues. You couldn't miss it if you tried."

"I don't know what it was …" Airsing mused as he glanced from Zayin to Xavier, hoping they would be quick to an answer.

Try it.

Syocer's eyes quickly flashed through his mind.

He steadied the blade, as he wielded the sharp tool, not too uncertain of what to do next.

"Lumos!"

A light fled the tip, drawing through the wooded path and throwing him down, as his blade clambered to the ground.

"Quite a recoil! I remember my father telling me of the 'miracles of dragons'," Zayin recalled as he helped Airsing to his feet.

"He said it was too much for one man to muster, but together the rider and dragon can stand strong in the midst of adversaries with this ability."

Zayin now ducked under a branch as he brushed the leaf-filled skies above him from view.

The bread and grains were a great find in Airsing's sac as Zayin's catch was taken into a soup; altogether, they were favorably content with their dinner. Airsing and Syocer found that the strength provided from the food was of great comfort, relieving their achy wounds.

After the fire was out, they found a good place to catch some sleep for the night.

"Who's on first watch?"

Xavier sprawled out beneath a tree as he fixed his head into his hands.

"I'll go first …" Xavier complied with his rhetoric as he settled even more deeply into the tree.

Miracles of dragons ... Syocer hummed as her eyes danced once more.

Rider, I have a story for you...your story...you need rest. It will find you in your sleep.

Airsing fumbled, out of exhaustion it seemed, onto the ground as Syocer flattened herself against the grassy earth, dwindling on the edge of lassitude herself. As his head relaxed on Syocer's back, he suddenly dripped into her memories.

18

Hope In A Stone

"Soren!" a woman's tone cut through the dark woods.

"He has to go," the man's voice found her ears, sternly, yet carefully backing his decision's finality.

"We might not come back."

Her brow furrowed as she yelped those last words, wrapping the small bundle around her gaze.

The man was a suitable height, with light, chestnut hair that folded over his ears. His facial features were aptly defined, though at places they were harshly jutting out.

The woman's gentle, yet beautiful eyes took in her surroundings as her blackening hair fell along her high cheekbones, finding her shoulders.

"Life is a small journey, where you can choose to have an influence…In this world, there's hopelessness…except for this."

He held out a small object as he smiled, "It's worthy of everything we have."

Her tears fell to the ground at his words; she closed her eyes as another one draped along her eyelashes. She turned, and as she did, the small bundle was brought out into the light; she tenderly pulled back a piece of the cloth to take in the picture that she might never see again.

"My boy ..."

The child blinked one eye as he felt the sun; as he did, the object glared a small spark as it was placed near him.

His mother quickly covered him up as they ran among the trees.

The forest looked strangely familiar.

"He's safe," Soren reassured her as they came to the child's grandfather; she quickly gave her son over to the man with reluctant anguish in her disposition.

He was younger and had brown hair then, even though it was interrupted with small splashes of white.

A lady held onto his arm, eyes wrinkling in sadness as she took the bundle from him. He grasped his daughter's shoulder tenderly; his eyes sparkled in despondency as she cast her hood down to reveal her one pointed ear, hugging Soren's father.

"Hope."

She quickly glanced at her son, then back to her father, only leading to the reappearance of her sullen eyes as she ran into the forest.

Time was sifting away.

The stone grew dark, seemingly out of the lack of amity it once felt so present before itself, as it was separated from the child.

"Soren, they'll be here by sundown."

"They won't find the boy…or the egg."

The man hurriedly took out a knife; he cut a leaf off of a tree and wrapped the egg inside of it.

He whispered a word, incomprehensible, as the leaf sparked and furled into a white inferno; the fragments drifted into the wind.

The sun took its leave from the orange horizon, interspersed by a blemished blue, as their footsteps flew along the ground.

A white flash then jumped through the sky, as the sparks disintegrated into an army that surrounded the man and woman.

"Soren," a gruff voice seized the crisp air as the Syfrin's hand reached out, now materializing.

"You search, you fail, Syros."

"You dirty scoundrel, where is it?" the Syfrin's voice hastened as he jumped from his horse, keeping his blade from driving into his opponent with little self-discipline.

"Kill me; you won't find it."

Soren threw his swords indignantly through the brush as they stood in the cruel ground; his hands were confidently poised at his side as they broke his blades, crushing them with their heels.

"Lower your dagger m'lady."

The woman wedged her blade into the ground as she leered into the Syfrin's brazen features. Her black hair now shockingly portrayed her searing eyes behind its shadows.

"Bind them: they won't give here."

The Syfrin sheathed his solemn blade with a growing thirst.

The woman gave Soren a quick glance of relief and at the same time, apprehension.

She was stationed in the front with spears stuck in her frail sides and back in case of resistance. Soren was in the back with the same treatment, except a rope about his neck.

"What do you suppose he'll do?" a Syfrin tantalized by her ear.

"Stranglle, tortttturrre, deattttth?"

Her face was solemn and unchanged as she tried to keep her focus, narrowing her eyes about the untried paths that led her feet.

You have glory in an instant, but what will you get in the future? she began, resting her mind on countless memories and hopes to parry their words; her eyes roamed far away from them as her lips were creased in a small smile.

19

Awake

"Where is it?" a dark voice cooled the very warmth in the army's bones.

"In the right hands." Soren stood firm, despite the cringing army behind him.

"Once more, where is the egg?"

The man leapt up, covertly hiding something, as he crept across the room. As he came to Soren, his voice settled into a state of dismal monotony.

He pointed a jagged, yet strong finger as his eyes cracked, seemingly made of ice.

"You."

"Yes," Soren took great care to question his captor's position.

"Who?" stated more as a command than a question.

"One only knows."

The dark voice flowed from the hooded creature, never wavering, "Would you like to play games? I'll play games."

His eyes grew overcast, like a storm about to take form.

"Guard...blade."

The warrior's blade was torn from his servant's hilt.

"Do you think a mere blade can force an answer when no fear lies in the eyes of your enemy?"

"You think of killing...how foolish…my thoughts are not yours ..."

Soren's eyes searched Arkt's intentions, as his pupils grew dark, swinging the blade playfully in and out of sight.

"Do what you will, but you can't harm it."

Arkt's grip was angrily thrust into Soren's side and slowly drawn out. Soren's eyes paled for a moment, and at the sight of blood, the man grew darkly satisfied; his joy rushed over the imbrued blade as his fingers ran through the crimson now falling across his palm.

The woman's brow furrowed; she took hold of Soren's shoulder with her tied hands as a guard quickly yanked her from him, casting her onto the floor. She nimbly struggled to get up as a stream of blood trickled down from a sharp gash by her eyes; she wiped it from her sight as she sneered, sighing confidently.

Soren's eyes developed in enmity; when he realized this, he turned them toward his captor.

"You don't like the lady's fate ..."

Arkt thrust his blade into her ribs as she gasped for breath, her sight fading.

"Take me," Soren cried helplessly, kneeling.

"No, this is good."

"Take me …" his voice grew shallow and noticeably dropped, callow as a fresh wind opening itself to the dying fall.

"Recant, repent, and reveal-then you can go easily."

"No, I…will not-" her voice wavered for a moment, then steadied, as she held her head high, gazing above Arkt's calm conduct; her lips trembled as her eyes shuddered, trying as hard as they could to mask the severe pain. Tears now cumulated in her eyes, glistening over the fullness of her mask's susceptibility.

Arkt forced his sword further into her as her whole frame shook, repelling, yet detained by the snickering guards.

"One only knows!" the woman's intonation proclaimed; her hair quickly whipped from her eyes, betraying her calloused expression as she writhed in the blade's throbbing intensity.

Soren enveloped her in his arms as he resisted the tug in his rope. He peered upon the gnarled frame as she tried to whisper, barely moving her lips. Soren steadily hushed her as her sight closed tightly away from the blinding darkness, lingering there for a moment as the blade fled from her side.

"I'm sorry ..." she mustered as her eyes slowly fluctuated from opened to closed.

"No...no," he silenced her wavering as she looked faintly back up toward Arkt, whose eyes were black with satisfaction.

The captor then allowed for a peace with a wave of his hand, his paces now echoing away from his prey.

"Lauck t'em en tha glrave. Thay caun't 'elp. Thay're aunly ae 'indrance," a guard yelped in a thick, Xav accent.

Swords and whips now clashed their skin. Soren tried to take the blows as he wrapped his bondage around her, his arms slashed in blood.

"Soren!" echoed off into the distant memories.

20

The First Flame

"Airsing," Xavier's voice was as clear as the flame penetrating the darkness; Airsing jolted upward, trying to keep his focus steady as his eyes adjusted to the light of the ascending sparks.

"What was it?" Zayin inquired, sitting by the fire and feeding a piece of kindling every so often to the wooden embers.

Tell them.

"My parents suffered…because of me," his last words heightened and dropped, as did his eyes onto the grass he now ruffled with his fingers.

Xavier, then standing, now made his way silently over toward Zayin as the two made eye contact, inquiring of Airsing by their glares.

His eyes hid deeply in the flames as he conveyed the story.

"…to spite their enemies ..." Zayin began as Syocer blew white, swirling smoke from her snout.

"Syocer...and them…they were the only ones who knew and …" Xavier contemplated whether or not to continue.

"Hmm?"

Zayin's brow furrowed as he stuck a piece of grass in his mouth, twiddling the end with his thumb and forefinger.

"What…was the Syfrin's name?"

Xavier's ears had heard right the first time, though he didn't want to remember.

"Syros."

Xavier's eyes fled the revealing sparks. For a moment, he seemed like a statue waiting under the mercy of his enemy.

"That was…my father …" he said, in each breath holding his head in his hand or wiping his brow, wanting to rip the memory from his mind.

"…That's not you…remember? You took a greater path, a narrow one, which none of them have been able to discover," Zayin consoled with his eyes on Xavier, catching his shoulder with his strong hand; the blade of grass now fled his mouth.

"As far as I know, he's still alive. They probably thought I was dead, until Duma and the others in Riv found us. They know *you're* alive, Airsing…which will alter their plans," his wavering voice halted as his silence paved the way to questions.

"Who else knew, Xavier?"

"Few Shilen...though, not anymore since their thoughts have been so long askew; they've nothing to remember…That's why we were attacked in the beginning…Arkt kept us veiled from the reality of it all …"

"Did your father ever mention anything about the war?"

"He said one-" his voice cut off as a white spark jolted above the trees.

"Shoot!"

Zayin heard Xavier cast down the wood and pick up his bow. He now threw the others their blades.

"Airsing, we need to reach Ryervy; if we get there too late, they'll cut us off from Kiren."

"They've seen you in the sky once too many times; you can't take that chance again…if you do, they'll be here in a matter of seconds," Zayin's voice collided with Xavier's.

"I'll be right behind you …" Xavier yelled as he inspected the white spark now raining into the forest; it seemed to be accompanied by something else that was too unfamiliar to remember at present.

They ran until their tracks hit the river, now rushing under the dwindling reflection of the moon. Syocer's wings propelled across the flowing rapids.

As they came to the mountains, a Syfrin appeared along with five others armed to kill.

"Look, there's Syros's boy. Never would have recognized him, except he has his *father's eyes*."

Xavier came running along; his bow was held tautly above his shoulder, eyes reddening as the Syfrin meddled with his emotions.

"I daun't," his Shilen accent relapsed into an intish state as Xavier firmly resented their comment.

He drew his arrow, testing it in the air.

"Who's first?"

The Syfrin glared at him as the leader remarked: "All of us, boy. Syfrin don't play fair. You should know; you are one."

"No…yuu shauld know whum you're dealing with…naut of Syfrin blud…now, thaut's dangeroussss boys …" Xavier balanced his arrows in his gaze, confidently parrying their words.

Syocer jumped, poised on her hind legs, as her talons ripped at the air, her scales bleeding heat. She growled as their attention diverted for a moment.

Her teeth sharpened, lengthening at a rapid pace, as Airsing remembered, "Sucöf!"

His mind faded into darkness as Syocer's nostrils blew out billowing smoke. Her mouth was a clear passage of white fire for an instant, enough to disperse them into ash.

21

Pure Fire

"Did you-?" Xavier's mouth lingered cracked in amazement as he still kept a hold on his perched arrow and bow.

"Fire-"

"My father said it took his dragon ages to breathe fire."

"That's no ordinary dragon; you're amazing!"

Syocer looked up as Airsing acknowledged her great accomplishment. His grin gave light to his pupils that were now searching the road before them; his eyes were fabricating blurry apparitions, trying to recreate the clear vision he had seen moments before.

"What else can you do?"

"She's not a dog, Xavier."

Zayin sheathed his sword as he cautiously looked about.

"Yeah, but you said something about 'dragon miracles'."

Xavier waved his hands up in the air as he clutched his hair, his Shilen accent coming back into his tongue.

"And *you* said something about the war."

Xavier's eyes focused mockingly on Zayin as he was obliged to continue: "...Syros said something about the trees becoming alive as the moon turned to darkness, the earth shaking, fearful of the next day."

They climbed the path as Xavier crouched to examine the land.

"The only light will be the stars in the sky reflecting off the swords and armor. The battle has no time or place...He said something like that. I barely remember...nor want to ..." he muttered the last to himself.

"Speaking of light, what were those white sparks? I've been meaning to ask that for a while now."

Airsing scratched his head, more out of the confusion of his sight than anything else, now looking for an answer.

"A signal of the Syfrin. Usually they've killed or found something."

"Seems they're always finding something, but can never keep a hold of it ..."

"Pretty dense creatures at times…except, there is Arkt…he's not of the Syfrin race of course…Another dimension's creatures are harder to escape from than these…These, well, they just don't know what makes them stumble when they fall."

Xavier recollected the inundating past he had to bear for so long as he looked back to make sure they were hidden from the view of the forest, which was now awakening under the colorful flicks of the sun.

All this time, they were walking upon the rugged terrain into the haze-filled mountains; Airsing pulled out the map, familiarizing himself with the dark etches on the parchment.

He ran his thumb across the ink as he glanced up, holding his sight on the sparse shade of the trees, interspersing the pathway on both sides.

"Ryervy's leagues away; we better start climbing."

"Something tells me we shouldn't. Stay close and be quiet…See these marks?"

Xavier's hand moved from rock to rock, sweeping across the unnatural scratches marred into the stones. A long growl, like the one back in the grave depths of Nyros, trekked toward the ringing echo of their footsteps.

Xavier's eyes quickly closed.

"You've never heard that sound before...If you have, you've seen the cruelty of Nyros."

He drew in a hard breath as he tried to silence it, nostrils flaring and eyes filling with memories of only a few days ago.

"They led us right into a trap. Airsing, whatever you do, get out of here *alive*."

"Xavier-?" Airsing clutched his shoulder as he steadily worked through Xavier's worry.

"It has no name known to the light dwellers. It hunts, kills, and destroys your very soul if you let it. In Nyros, they called it the apocalypse Syfeklen. You have no idea what it's like to look into the eyes of that creature."

The cry grew until even the rocks ran from the heights, fumbling upon their feet as they were now struggling to stand against the colossal rubble sliding down the mountains.

Xavier tested the rock walls as he found a hollow thud. His head turned, ear meeting the surface of the unbreakable barrier as he tested it again in disbelief.

At that very moment, the shriek rang for ages until the valley was silent; all was still.

"It found its prey. Move!"

His steps were now tentative, though they seemed to be testing the ground in an energetic manner; he hopped along in a strange effort as he kept exploring every point of the sky.

Syocer searched the land as they followed Xavier's steps. They turned quickly into a crevice, as the ghost-like skull protruded from where they had originally stood.

With a huge rock in its terrestrial fangs, fresh blood fell from its mouth. The very nostrils blew fire into the air as it sniffed, and the body was immense as it sent the mountains trembling in fear.

The company now silently climbed through the rocks, anticipating the Syfeklen's actions as they winced at every dribbling rock falling from their efforts. The creature's steps stopped as Syocer's wings folded over Airsing's hand; her eyes collided with his as they portrayed a figure. He looked deeper into the reflection as he saw the creature itself.

It's the present.

Her pupils now reflected Airsing's eyes.

Xavier's grip on the mountain's edge faltered as he took a rock to the ground with him, falling into a muddy stream. He quickly looked up to see a small opening in the stone, delightfully invigorating his sense of hope.

All three peered over the edge to find he was all right, pointing to the aperture in the side of the mountain.

Abruptly, the whole face of rock shattered behind them, becoming like an avalanche on their heels; Xavier was the first to see it as he yelped for their attention.

Airsing grasped Syocer's tail as she flew off the edge, the creature appearing on the rocky shore.

The Syfeklen took in the fresh air, making it paralyzing to breathe, as its flame soaked the edges of the mountainous ruins, running toward their heels.

Zayin stumbled on the sliding rocks, but then regained his composure as he hunkered over to help Xavier to his feet, running all the while.

Syocer threw Airsing into the crevice; he hit the ground at the same time he was trying to sprint. Airsing saw the flames closing in on the cave as his head and limbs scraped the cavernous rocks. His legs willed him to run as he clambered back up on his soles, adrenaline too fired up to notice his scrapes.

Xavier yanked himself from the nerve-racking position he was in: flattened against the wall, mesmerized by the flames. Zayin yanked at his attention as he groped for any piece of clothing he could, Airsing yelling to get their focus past the ashen walls.

22

Channel Of Memories

The cave became nothing but tainted chaff from the flames as the three stood holding their heads up out of the sheer satisfaction that they were still standing.

Syocer.

Airsing's mind raced as the three settled on a wall, breathing choppy.

"Xavier, in Nyros…how did you control the creature…or kill it?" Airsing's mind was racing too fast to keep up with his tongue as he steadied himself onto his feet.

"To control it, they had to summon a sorcerer...I've never heard…of killing this thing. There's no way- …"

Xavier looked into his eyes, contemplating his next move. He couldn't help but notice a small glimpse of his own past in Airsing:

His mother bent down to look into his eyes; her thin hands were gingerly placed on his head as she held his features, soaking in this simple visage.

"Be strong…my boy."

Her eyes reflected his face more certainly as the glazing water pooled in the corners of her eyes. Her sight turned to blurry tears as she tried to brush them off, guards breaking into the house and tearing him into a realm of hopelessness.

"Look...hu …" letting out a sigh as he gripped Airsing's shoulder: "You are the only hope to this and the next generations who may *live* or *die* depending on your destiny…and that would be pretty poorly spent by being face to face with *that thing!*" pointing toward the cave's mouth, he displayed his righteous anger as his back straightened.

"Xavier, you can't-" Airsing stopped as he unleashed his blade, "Just trust me."

With that, he took his sword and fled from the cavern.

Xavier lunged for him, but was caught by something he couldn't see.

Syocer.

Airsing, stay inside. Don't...Airsing, trust me.

Airsing fell into the ominous stillness of the extent. Then, he heard a disturbance in the silence, as a rock stumbled from its place and fell behind him.

His hair stood on end as he saw a shadow, like water groping from rock to rock, sliding down upon the shaky grave.

The creature growled as the echo seemed to run in every direction; Airsing's ears were bleeding from the harsh noise. The beast took advantage of his shock and plunged toward him, Airsing evading its claws at the last moment as his balance was startled by the creature's landing. He looked up; everything seemed as if it was covered in armor, though he couldn't be too sure because his vision was now regressing back to a blurry picture. Regardless, Airsing slashed and pierced until the thing jumped, sending flames in his direction.

His clothes now singed, he hid behind a precipice of rock as he brushed the flames from his holey garb.

He grasped his sword again, looking up at the piece of metal through his wiry hair as he tried to figure a way out of this predicament.

As he readied himself against the rock's edge, the creature ran forward and cut back in an instant, finding him in his hiding place. The air was now fetid and void of breathable air as Airsing tried to stand; he now slid quickly away from the edge as the Syfeklen ran to tear him to pieces.

Then, he was conquered by a gust of wind and scales.

When will you learn?

His feet felt the cave's dank ground as Syocer's snout met his hand; Airsing was standing rigidly before her, nonetheless smiling at the very roughness of her scales in his gauntlet.

Where's Xavier and Zayin? she inquired as she looked around, eyes blinking in radiance.

"Looking for someone?"

Airsing turned, now seeing two red eyes of a grave appearance shadowing a garment's veil.

"Tell me where they are, and you can leave with your head."

Airsing's blade was confidently at his side as he gripped the hilt in his hand.

"Cocky," the Syfrin laughed.

He called his army into the light with a flick of his hands.

"Boy, you don't know who you're dealing with."

His grin ceased to lighten his eyes.

"I am Syros, leader of the king's armies. Yes…I know you've heard of me…He has sent me to you to kill you, torture you? No. Take you to him. He will do things far worse than these. Boy, you consider yourself lucky to have fallen into my hands."

"I don't believe in luck…and I've heard of your failure once before: what makes this time any different?"

Syros's movements seemed to halt upon Airsing's words.

"Boy, luck's the only thing you have left to believe *in*."

"You're wrong," his voice quietly settled the air as he smirked in the Syfrin's face; Syros's jaw was held taut as to not betray himself to his words.

Airsing, don't listen to him.

"Listen to me. Yes, I can hear your thoughts."

(Syros had a dragon long ago before Xavier was born when he was known as Phasen. The dragon was killed and sent Phasen into a horrible depression; this was all hidden from Xavier's knowledge. Phasen, when abducted to Nyros, forgot of his dragon and previous life. His keen senses, though still acute, are failing because of his dragon's absence.)

Nyr, ty tyrny clerf. Ty uth te synterf.[18]

Syocer's snarl presented itself in Syros's face with teeth held close and scent of flame behind the smoky breath.

"Wise is your dragon."

He tilted his head as if he wanted so much to plunge his sword into her heart.

"You are not able to understand us."

Terragon vyr a os.[19]

If I could kill you, I would. Your bloody parents ... Syros began as he smiled, inevitably giving way to his thoughts.

Lumos, ty tyrny clerf yawfy tir.[20]

"Kill me, then. You know you want to…receive the glory. The hope is lost, down to one single *thing*."

Airsing whipped his blade playfully out into his hands, now feeling that he had a little leverage with which to perplex the Syfrin.

"What are you talking about? No hope is left if you're dead."

Syros's eyes became a hot, glaring red once more.

Airsing's attention strayed to two figures, clothed in dark garments, silently coming to the front of the army.

"Lord Syrosss, the king is naut patient in killing matters," an intish accent spoke, although something seemed familiar about it.

The army left the cave as Airsing's chain was now connected up to Syocer's back wings, which were bound in tight shackles; her forewings were bent awkwardly into her back, throwing her balance slightly awry.

As they found their footing awkwardly on the path in front of them, Airsing now remembered how the hooded figure walked and then stared at him with: *Of course...green eyes held in red ...*

Syros, nor Airsing, hadn't recognized Xavier or Zayin*...especially not his son...Xavier would have been dead because of his treason.*

Syocer found this truth to be prevalent in his mind.

---

[18] Literal meaning: No, he cannot. He is an evil truth tongue.

[19] Literal meaning: Remain in the light.

[20] Literal meaning: Warrior's light, he cannot touch you.

Airsing slightly looked behind him, pretending to rest his eyes longingly on his freedom.

Zayin's posture gave him away, besides his ever-so-often slipping hood. Zayin carried the rope tied to Airsing as Xavier bore the shackles, followed by more Syfrin and chain possessors.

Xavier gave Airsing a look, which said it all: *Airsing, if we could run, we would, but there's no way out of this one until we get to Nyros. I promise you, I will find a way out. Trust me?*

Airsing and Syocer surveyed their thoughts in the Rader language, as the sun was now settling into the darkening ground.

Airsing caught a glimpse of Syocer's eyes as he glanced upward, noticing how clear they looked.

After traveling blindfolded through dripping caverns and curious places, they finally halted under the direction of silence. The black cloth fell from Airsing's eyes as Syocer was now peering into their blue antiquity; his pupils flicked back and forth as his brow fell into a gloomy furrow. Airsing stared into the city as the gate creaked open, full of darkening marks of evil. Clashes of hammers and tools ceased to ring as the wooden mechanisms flung across the vision; the floodgates of this portal were laid bare, dripping across their eyes.

The lead Syfrin yanked Airsing from his feet as Syocer blew smoke in his eyes, unthankful. Airsing's muscles tensed awkwardly as he got up, his feet twisting in the chains.

The Syfrin around the path spat, jeered, ridiculed, mocked, and beat Syocer and Airsing rigid; they kept standing, though weak as they were.

All the while, Xavier's grip tightened on his bow as tears came to his eyes at the sight; he remembered how much he hated this place and how much pain had become etched into him.

"Whoa, my friend. I have a plan," Zayin alighted, though Xavier's grip didn't relax.

The path stopped abruptly as a pitch-dark shadow came into view. The army parted as it grew nearer to Airsing, like ice-cold water trickling into a stream. Syocer, growling and bucking, flouted in the king's face.

He ignored the dragon as his eyes saw Airsing's fierce expression.

"I'm not afraid of you, and neither is she."

"You should be," a hard voice shook the air: "I'd consider you a fool."

Arkt grasped his sword. And waving the still tainted blade in Syocer's face, he reminded: "You know what your parents did before they died? So is your fate. Unless…you choose to recant and become a loyal follower…There are ways in which you will bow down gracefully…better than your parents could ever do."

Without hesitation, Airsing spat, "I will never help you, your army, or your plan." Airsing smirked, "I will kill you, mark my words, one day you will be dead."

Airsing's smile remained even till Arkt's next sentence, which greatly annoyed him:

"Not if I kill you first."

Arkt tightened his grip on the red sword as it struck Airsing's head. Blood spilt through Airsing's mouth as ice surged through his whole body.

Syocer's cry grew louder as Airsing's vision faded slowly into darkness.

Arkt bowed to meet his ears as he whispered, "You will be dead, even if I cease to exist …"

Syocer's scales felt rough, though greatly familiar under his hands.

They were locked in a lightless room.

Syocer?

Airsing, your will is strong.

Where's Arkt?

He said he would give you a cruel welcome when you came around...He seems to be lost to this world ...

Syocer's eyes were now flickering radiance across the damp floor as she shed the luminosity toward Airsing.

A hard clank hit the door as a foreign light pierced the darkness. Syocer, poised for attack, mustered Airsing to his feet.

"Airsing-?" whispered a familiar voice.

"Xavier."

23

By Blood

Xavier wrapped one arm around Airsing's shoulder as he kept his other hand on a blade he had picked up from the sentry guarding the door-or shall we say: was guarding the door.

He wiped it clean from the dusty ruins as he motioned for Syocer. They stepped over the ashen vestiges as Xavier explained that Zayin was clearing the exit.

"Here, take your sword."

Airsing was glad to have his blade back in his hand as he quickly sheathed it, following Xavier's steps that seemed so conversant with their surroundings.

The fresh air was a relief to the musty passages weaved inside the tower, as the moon now shone under the leaves of the trees, revealing the evening's still prevalent glare.

The camps of Syfrin were dousing the flames of rejoicing fires when the three moved through the brush undetected. Zayin met them in a nearby wooded passage, watching the shadows pitter across the lightless place; the traces of light seemed too scarce to find.

They were well out of range when the moon had fully reached its apex in the sky, the fires now quenched from their view.

"How convenient," a voice startled Zayin, but echoed as mundane as his pretentious colloquialisms could ever be into Xavier's wakening ears.

"If you kill him, you'll have to kill me," Xavier said, as he pushed his hood from his face, standing in direct opposition with Syros; Xavier's scarred features were even more evident in the moonlight as he unleashed his blade, expression doubtlessly unwavering.

Xavier shifted a swift cut toward him, as the Syfrin parried the blade.

Zayin's sword stopped abruptly as Xavier began, "He's mine," all the while keeping his eyes on Syros.

Xavier's sword sparked as he parried a sudden attack; he cut at the Syfrin's blade until he found a sword blanketing his own hand in blood. He cried stiffly as the Syfrin's grin grew lighter; Syros now jolted at him with his blade held high above his head, marking the last blow to Xavier's frame.

Xavier used all of his strength as he cut through the attack, the sharp edge now flying in pieces of shards as Xavier stood resolutely opposing his father.

"I am your son by blood ..."

He kept his sword by Syros's heart as he finished, "Your enemy by choice. Tell me now."

His father fell to the ground, speechless.

"You are mine to kill …"

Syros's mouth tightly clenched shut as his strong jaw forbade him speak, lest his life be lost at a quicker pace. Xavier stood in the clearing, peering through his father: his abusive, evil, insolent, murderous father.

Zayin looked up to see Xavier's concentrated, muscle-strained appearance.

Finally, he spoke: "Remember this ..."

Xavier held his blade readily as he remained steady, "I am not of you. I should kill you, but I don't…If you should ever cross our path again, your life will be taken…for it is *easily* taken…Phasen, remember how much your soul's worth …"

Zayin picked up the broken blade to ensure no backsliding from Syros, as Xavier, with his sword's hilt, pushed him back into the ground.

As he kept a mark on Syros with his blade point, they backed through the forest, Xavier wrapping his hand in his garment.

Their journey took them across the Zjy plain until they were out of the range of Esgaroth.

"Here isn't safe. We need to make it to the Mount Fortress," Xavier replied to their stillness, looking down at his tainted hand.

The once long and lingering silence dispersed as it forgot its waiting to be broken.

"When I was young, just taken captive by the Syfrin...he used to beat me…took me so close to death so many times, I didn't know whether I was still in the land of the living when I awoke the next morning...He told me I was the sun's shadow …

"You know, the strange thing-well, it's not strange now-it doesn't bother me anymore, but it used to."

He reflected on the memory and then threw it to the ground in a visual effort of a stone.

Zayin came up and placed his hand admiringly upon Xavier's shoulder.

"Wow…that's just it…it isn't enough to say …" which was the only thing he could find to show his great awe and respect for this young warrior with an old soul.

"Nothing, but a change…There was only hopelessness back there...I saw some Shilen and others around had a light in their eyes."

He stationed his foot upon a large rock as he ripped his shirt, wrapping the cloth firmly around his palm.

"I wanted that light, the one you have, more than anything."

Now that the bandage was enfolded over his palm's gash, his leg slid quickly from its perch.

"I don't know of anyone who has it more …" Airsing responded as the sun fled the mountaintops, pointing to Xavier, who was smiling underneath his white hair.

The colorless sky seemed to envy the mountains, which became brighter in greens and blues with an occasional mist peppering the canyons.

"Wait-we just passed Illu."

Zayin tried to recall the area as his memory availed.

"Could I see your map?"

"Sure."

Airsing gripped the parchment as it softly crumbled in his gauntlet.

Zayin was now mouthing directions as he looked toward the sky, then at the charred article.

Suddenly, his eyes familiarized themselves with his memory as they gave way to certainty.

"Follow me…hear those tracks? They're on our tail…follow here…I'll show you something...One thing isn't on this map …"

24

Standing On Air

"My father found this place. He said the dragon riders are rightly equipped to open the passage...He took me in it once."

His eyes brightened once more as he felt the scars on the trees, retracing his long ago past.

"Here it is."

He peered beyond the treetops as the mountain gave way to a canyon filled with colors beyond their regular hues.

The canyon was marked by the mist, which reflected the colors around it by the sun. (When in flight, the mist makes it visible as a plateau engraved in the mountains.)

Zayin led the way to a sharp turn.

"Here. He used to say…something…a certain word ..."

Try.

Yintary mith[21], unsure of his words, he spoke.

Syocer's thoughts fused with Airsing's as a quake collapsed the ground beneath their feet. They didn't fall, but were standing on air. Xavier looked down for a moment, seeing the reflection of himself watching his every move; he smiled at his white hair as he proceeded to move his sight upon his green eyes.

---

[21] Literal meaning: Open alive.

Syocer journeyed into the stone-hewed opening, as the others followed. The ground was clear, reflecting as water to sky.

"What is this?"

"My father called it Took wayaelf. He said it was a passage to hope for something and find it."

Used for dimensions ... Syocer's voice trailed off as Airsing meant to ask, but failed to do so when, abruptly, footsteps rushed upon their attentive ears.

Zayin motioned silence.

The steps didn't cease as the tunnel felt like it was crumbling upon their frames. What seemed like dust now fell from the sky of this place, precipitating on their clothes as they peered tentatively upward. The firmament of the cavern was raining upon them.

Their attention fell from the droplets as Syocer found Airsing's eyes when a faint tone yelled, "Find him: no mercy!"

The voice was noticeably the leader, but Xavier thought it strange that it was untried to his ears.

Zayin silently sped through the dark crossing, spurred by a vague sight, when, finally, the steps diminished to nothing. The company followed him, finding shelter from the misty ruins of this tunnel.

Refreshingly, a cool wind engulfed the four who looked at the source expectantly; the gelid droplets had ceased to fall.

As the memory was relived back in Nyros, Zayin stated, "You know, back there, I thought you were dead."

"So far, I've been dead to everyone at least once."

Zayin brushed Airsing's hair into a mess as they kept a good pace.

"You like to do that a lot," he referred to his hair, moving along the tunnel.

"Arkt's thirst for torture left him with nothing." Zayin disregarded his words about the hair bit.

As the crisp air dodged the turns of the tunnel, it halted and loomed in the atmosphere when a burst of sunlight crushed through the surface; the ray shone in an eerie radiance.

"Let's see where Syocer took us."

As the darkness no longer engulfed their senses, the light emerged freely into their eyes.

The land was awesome with mountains behind and in front. The valleys were filled with green growth and rivers; a plateau emerged from the rough terrain as it dropped, overlooking a forest.

"Whoa."

Xavier shaded his eyes in an effort to receive the whole scene in its crisp clarity.

Everlasting mountains.

25

Chance In A River

Airsing, we need to go quickly...Today is the seventh day.

"We have to reach the forest."

Zayin was now smiling, "There's one way...it's dangerous ..."

Xavier spoke first: "The river," he begrudged as if he was a cat to water.

Zayin ran ahead as he stepped onto the plateau, looking down upon the spectacle.

"You'll have to swim."

"Shilen weren't gifted with *swimming* as much as...*fighting*," Xavier piped up, trying to seek another possibility.

Zayin peered in his direction as if saying, "What else have we got?"

Consequently, Xavier was the first in the river. The tide was swift with many currents and jagged rocks. In a few moments, Xavier was far from sight.

Next, Syocer sped through the water as Airsing trailed behind her current.

Hold on, Rider.

His eyes lit as he grasped her tail; the current picked up through the icy water, granting his muscles with the right to quiver. A large rapid took Airsing under as he held Syocer's tail, now fully immersed in the frost. His frame rashly broke the surface as his hair dripped so slowly with the glassy globules.

From there Syocer soared from the long waterfall, Airsing flipping toward her as he tried to catch her tail.

"Woo hoo!" Airsing's voice trailed past the rushing rapids.

As they went down the fall, he saw his reflection catching onto Syocer's, where they were mirrored in the cascading threads entwined in the water. The wind now brushed Airsing's eyes closed, leaving him trying to overcome the force that held them there. He managed to crack his eyes, seeing a few, small droplets slowly dithering upward as they flexed their round forms, wavering until they would impart a cool bliss upon his skin.

The river ran too rapidly to enjoy the sights as it drew along to forever, it seemed. When the tide began to subside, the sun was already hanging along the back ridges of the mountains.

"Cool, but refreshing."

Xavier smiled as he shook his silver hair, now spiking into its normal position and gleaming white as the sun hit the beads of water resting gingerly on the threads of his brow.

Zayin ran from the water as he grabbed Xavier's sword, facing the hilt in his hand.

"Keep that...There…Reshen Mountains."

Curtly, he moved on, wary of their surroundings, but more so of time.

As they reached the peak of the mountain, Airsing peered over the edge; nothing was visible until: *Sucöf.*

As soon as his vision zoomed into the Red Plain, he saw legions of Syfrin and Xav.

"Airsing," Zayin cautioned, diverting his attention, as they turned toward a poorly fortified city, taken long ago by the warriors as a fortress.

Syocer? Airsing inquired of the still, deserted fortification.

Only the Shilen army's left.

The stones didn't make a sound as their feet met the rocks; all was silent. The birds had left the sign of nature's warning: stillness, but not of peace.

"They've been waiting for you, Airsing…They've read the signs," Zayin's tone broke the ominous suspicions.

A man, clad in armor and on his horse, jumped from his saddle with something like a new light in his eyes. The four bowed until he quickly rebuked them.

"No, don't bow...please...you'll disgrace my humility! Believe me, you stand...Rider, dragon, and companions."

He took off his helmet, revealing a fairly elderly man, his white hair giving a pleasant contrast to his olive skin and silvery-brown eyes. He extended his hand, seeming to take in the whole of the sight before him.

"'Tis my honor, Rider. My name is Tsadhe."

"This is Syocer, Xavier, and Zayin...I'm Airsing."

He smiled, almost forgetting himself in the whole equation.

"Zayin? Are you Saber's boy?"

Zayin looked up as his features alighted, incredulously veiled from the details.

"You knew my father?"

"I fought alongside him in the battle of Rivensky...Honorable man. He died right before my eyes...I held his dragon's head as he diminished into dust ..." he recalled as the countenances of the company became short of contrary, allowing the king to speak; his own eyes were gravely poised, fluctuating by his words.

"I knew him for only a short time ..."

The king's eyes faded into crescent moons, sparkling.

"We have a few Shilen ..." King Tsadhe looked in Xavier's direction, "...to fight, but we need more soldiers. Their stronghold has been emptied."

"How many are we?" Xavier inquired, raising his head, sarcastically hopeful of the size of the army.

"Right now...three hundred. Nyros has five thousand strong. Though, judging their disposition...they will kill their own to get to you."

"How thirsty are they?"

"Son, glory means more to them than *life*. You on the other hand," he turned from Zayin to Airsing, then strayed into Syocer's eyes, "...have learned that when surrounded by acclamations of every kind, to be steadfast...and as a consequence, full of humility and given to the right of action."

26

Visible Air

"Rider, our swords are on your side," Tsadhe stated as he gravely peered into the plain.

"No matter the outcome ..." he whispered the last part mostly to himself as to not minimize the morale of the troops.

"Thank you, sir, that's devout-"

"-But we need help." Xavier's tone cut through, picking up where Airsing lacked, as he offered up suggestions: "Their army is coming straight here, so Syocer can fly to surrounding allies and gather more soldiers."

"I'm afraid time is too short."

"No, sir-I've seen her fly...she's faster than the wind," Zayin began.

You ready?

You heard him, Syocer...there's not enough-

You just hang on ...

Syocer grasped Airsing by her talons and swiftly swung him on her back, too quickly for him to object.

Airsing, you won't be able to see a thing. Sucöf.

The blurry wind raced with Syocer's wings when, suddenly, the earth became clear and light; the gusts were stabilized as Syocer scattered the pixilated clouds with her talons.

The first reinforcement is there.

She focused her claw on a point, too blurry to make out at present.

The Elven range halted unexpectedly to Airsing's view, as Syocer landed almost silently before the doors of the Elven king's army.

The knights froze in fearful awe as their armor now trickled with the uncertain fires that graced the night.

Courage has left their eyes as well as their hearts. We should send them far instead of into battle.

Airsing, they're the only army in this region. You will find that one with a steadfast heart performs well under these circumstances; this is all we have for now ...

He looked onto the glazed stones as the Elven lord ran from the doorway, clad in armor.

"Sir, I have no time to explain, but we need your armies at the Fortress."

"Rider, we will be of your services," the Elven king stated as he drew his sword solemnly through the air.

"You are the last chance…we have fought for centuries to keep it safe…we will do the same here," his eyes reflected the knowledge of the ancient entity, namely hope.

They flew into the sky as the army ran beneath the shadow of Syocer's spanned appendages.

Then, Airsing became aware of his position: upside-down and moving quickly.

Stay on, Syocer laughed as her talon gripped him, spiraling through the wind.

Fly as fast as you can.

I will when you get up.

He climbed until he clasped her back wings, gripping them with a tight alacrity that made him focus on how cold his palms felt as they tingled with an invigorating sensation of the moisture that shrouded the atmosphere.

Hold on.

Sucöf.

The wind was now visible as she soared past the almost stable air.

The wind is stationary...How fast are you going? That's amazing ...

Airsing narrowed his eyes, which were now fixed below her moving body as he felt like they were even racing past the rays of the sun's paces.

Not as amazing as you think ... she paused for a moment, soaking in the thinning gleams of the tapering sun that became like a flame to their view.

Your father was an amazing man, yet never gave light to his power...except when he needed to use it...for that is what made him amazing.

Her eyes sparkled in a humble "thanks" as Airsing's mind raced through the clouds, breaking into the familiar plains of Arithmere. Airsing's attention watched the Syfrin on the ground as Syocer easily dodged their arrows.

Airsing's vision grew more acute, acclimating to the speed, as he looked past the plain into the Passage of Thela.

Airsing, we need to turn back...they've been overtaken.

Syocer flipped and jetted past the clouds.

27

Focusing On Wind

As Syocer's muscles held onto the breeze, Airsing felt the moment take him. As her speed left the wind in a state of shock, Airsing raised his arms.

The air stream was pushing him back like a hard rush of water caressing a stone in its force. He quickly pushed his arms to Syocer's scales, her frame speeding up into the gusts.

The air flew through his hair like something so indescribably refreshing as he crouched behind her wings. The crisp smell flooded his senses as the very atmosphere yanked his breath far away, invigorating his whole being.

She sheathed her wings as they penetrated the very atmosphere that held them; everything was a perfect white as Syocer's scales reflected this nature.

His shirt was a flag in the rush as Syocer dove through the clouds; every inch of him was penetrated by the cool ambiance.

He was weightless, on a different sphere of existence, though everything embodied the familiarity so evidently spurting past them; it was like a tail of a meteor was raining about this star's intensity.

He smiled as Syocer gave him a ride. Her growl rumbled through all the earth, warning the troops for battle.

She spiraled into a wind tunnel, everything blurry except for the focus.

28

One Thousand To Five Thousand

Syocer's wings folded as Airsing ran into the ground, dizzy from the flight. His heart was beating too quickly to measure as his energy was revived; he now wiped his nose from a trickle of blood that had begun to form from the lack of oxygen present in the atmosphere.

Syocer whipped her scales as the jump created a catapult for the very fine specks of mist laden in the rivets. Airsing became aware that his clothes were thinly dusted with vapor as he leapt up from his state of exhilarating shock.

"You just left," Xavier mused expectantly, as if this was regularity.

"Does faster than wind explain anything?" Xavier started again as Airsing stumbled upon his feet.

Syocer whipped her wings for balance as she leapt into the turret overlooking the plain.

"Sir, where do we stand?"

"With the Elven, one thousand to five thousand."

"One thousand few to five thousand strong."

"Don't forget Syocer."

Zayin sturdily placed his hand on Xavier's shoulder as he stated, "She's worth far more than five thousand ..."

"We've come with you this far; we're not about to let you down...We're right behind you, death or life."

Xavier cupped his bow in his hand, alleviating an arrow from its perch and twirling it about in a versatile flick of his fingers as he watched the plain through the flashes of the feather.

"It's a while before they cross the plain, and the Elven are close."

"Equip yourselves; you can't go into battle with cloth to protect you."

The king threw armor into their hands.

Airsing took his armor off as quickly as he had donned it.

"Too bulky, I can't move in this."

"Take mine, Rider."

"No, you're the one on the ground."

"You're more important; you have to be kept alive."

There was no hint of mockery in Xavier's tone as Airsing peered upon the end of his outstretched arm.

"No, Xavier."

Syocer backed Xavier off with a puff of smoke as she calmly and still humbly gleamed her prerogative.

Xavier turned his words toward Syocer, "Yeah, you're both alike: hard headed."

Syocer's exhale wisped into Airsing's drying hair as he tied his boot strings taut.

The Elven army was stationed around the defending walls. Their bows were, with ease, ready to shoot with the steady arch of the wood resting upon their armor.

The Shilen were ranked a step behind them in an effort to kill if the Syfrin or Xav scaled the walls.

Flames were set afire as the whole scene grew nervously tranquil, if such a phrase can be understood.

The door was barred with rocks and iron, finishing the preparation.

The surroundings seemed surreal as the sun disappeared, the moon never climbing its familiar path to light the sky; the stars glared ever brighter and ran off the tips of the metals silently awaiting their fate.

"Xavier," whispered Airsing.

"What?"

"Did you say the trees came alive?"

A long groan, like a crack of a limb falling, collapsed upon their ears as Xavier nodded.

A growl came billowing over the top of the mountain.

29

Ryden A Cur

I'm ready when you are.

"Xavier, I'll need your confidence."

Airsing jumped over the wall, clutching Syocer's back wings as he crouched behind her long neck.

As Syocer raced through the beginning of a jagged downpour, Airsing kept his keen vision alive so he could easily make out their course.

The forest neared their sight as Airsing looked up into the visible droplets raining like stars on the earth. The leaves were dithering slightly as the small specks drizzled and jumped from the greenery.

Airsing leapt from Syocer's back, landing on the untouched earth. Seemingly at a standstill, the woods groaned in the wind as the canopy parried the rain from the ground.

"How're we going to reach them all?" his voice filled the air and was taken by the gusts floating eerily through the dark trails that were fabricated by the entwined branches of the depleted trees.

His eyes met Syocer's as she bowed her head to the forest.

"Ryden a cur[22] …"

---

[22] Literal meaning: Ride the wind.

His message climbed throughout each bough of bark and leaves until a startling rush of wind hit Airsing's features.

"We wrill farrllorw yroukkkkk." The barky feel of the tongue crept into his ears.

Airsing mounted Syocer as the soft earth fled from her claws.

As soon as Airsing glimpsed back into the dark forest, the roots of the trees were moving into an army like a torrent of clouds forming for a tornado.

The trees ran in a rapid pace, roots lunging before them, as Airsing felt Syocer's claws and tail rudder their course.

The Syfrin army had already begun to advance into the battleground, as the trees ran through the Red Plain, climbing the mountain before them in a moment.

Syocer's claws rested on the mountain's rocky terrain as the very ground quickly fled into the midst of the war, tree branches and roots crushing through the mountain itself.

Ten thousand strong more like.

"Ryviandier![23]" Airsing yelled as the trees poured over the mountain, towering over the Syfrin and surprising them from the back.

Airsing crouched once more upon Syocer's neck scales as he readied his muscles for flight.

Ever step of the trees crushed the soldiers as if they were nothing but chaff in the wind.

As Syocer flew above the war, she dodged each arrow, diving down to disperse white flame into the legions of Syfrin, though not lingering even for a moment.

The downpour ensued nothing but dark distress as the waking night was now transformed into an unknown reality.

Syocer dodged and ducked under trees and arrows as she spun through the sky. Airsing's legs escaped the sureness of her back once as she tumbled through the blurry barrages of arrows, his palms cupping her wing sockets.

Airsing now held her appendages within his gauntlets as he took his own hand at arrows, his knees steadying Syocer's forewings as well as balancing himself upon the wind.

---

[23] Literal meaning is one that is most closely related to the English word: Run! (Deciphered from the tongue of the trees: more commonly known as Arundelian.)

Zing!

Zayin cut another Xav's grappling hook from scaling the walls. He turned quickly to see a Syfrin leaping at him with his sword poised awkwardly across his stature. The Syfrin clambered to the ground as a bow's feather protruded from his armor. Zayin peered up quickly, his fingers still tied to his hilt, seeing Xavier's frame make up the background of the explanation.

"Close one," Xavier's rhetoric appeared void of a troubled demeanor as his eyebrows were now raised in jest.

"Yeah," Zayin began, suppressing his excited exhale, half expecting another Xav to come abruptly upon him.

Xavier pivoted quickly, aiming for the ground; his sight flooded over the many Syfrin trying to scale the walls. As Xavier took a few arrows from his quiver, sizing up the bunch, a Syfrin clutched his shoulders, hindering his already projected arrows from meeting their marks.

Zayin cut through to the Syfrin as Xavier tried in an effort of defense, driving an arrow into his head. This stunned the captor momentarily, enough to allow the blade of Zayin to plunge directly into Xavier's view, being a true shot as the soldier disintegrated. Xavier dusted the Syfrin's paws from his shoulders as be brought out his sword, looking back toward the smiling Zayin.

"Payback can never come too soon ..."

"Thanks ..." Xavier gasped, smiling into the midst of some rushing Syfrin.

Zayin and Xavier clashed blades and covered the other's direction as Xavier kept his bow in his quiver, though not too far from his hand.

Syocer flew closer to the ground as Airsing wielded his sword; he was now crouching upon her back and parrying attacks.

Syocer sped into the air as a tree fell behind her, Airsing now holding onto her forewings.

We need to push the Syfrin closer to the city.

With pleasure.

She plummeted through the foliage as more trees poured over the mount.

Syfrin were trying to escape the war, cringing in every effort to evade the barky behemoths and scale the mountain's wrath, only to fall backward into the midst of the devastating limbs and roots that devoured them in cracks.

Airsing found Syocer's thoughts as his vision became nothing short of blurry; the atmosphere developed into darkness as leaves clambered upon his frame.

Sucöf.

The light from Syocer's mouth grew as white as lightning as it struck the ground and ran through the plain.

One Syfrin had taken advantage of this short breath and shot Airsing in his leg.

Airsing quickly looked down, and upon throwing his dagger, the Syfrin dispersed into ash; he cringed as he broke the arrow from his knee, now winding his garment tightly around the wound as he began to notice how cold his shaking muscles were.

Airsing now shot many arrows through the shroud, lest even more come barraging upon Syocer's wings and his skin as they flew into the sky.

Syocer?

As her talons released the dirt, beginning to fly, her wings were clipped by the overriding arrows. Airsing fell from her back as her flight pattern wavered. She quickly plummeted to the ground as she caught him just before the fall, taking the brunt of the crash herself as she shielded Airsing with her wings.

His senses felt a force of failing light cracking around him.

Syocer was dying.

He ran from her protection as his sword cut the air.

"Lumos Syer![24]" gusts of white swirls gave light to his breath as the wind died down in their midst, giving way to the spectacle that followed; Airsing's form was emanating with bright sparks of light as the droplets of water no longer lingered across his drenched body.

His light fled the field as the Syfrin lay in ash; an apocalyptic radiance swept through the plain, gently laying the enemies to rest as the scene became surreal. The ashes rose as the stars gleamed in satisfaction, an aurora dancing upon the stillness. Dust seemed to peacefully ordain the wind as the blinding light fled like a wave resounding upon the shore. Nothing had ever been so bright. Trees bowed and slowly swayed back and forth as if they were being knocked about in the wind.

---

[24] Literal meaning: Warrior's light weapon!

Syocer's limbs were now shaking as she managed to hold her head above the ground, eyes bright, yet glazed over. Airsing rocked back into the reality of the battlefield that was now glistening with dusty clouds as he felt the light around him fade, beads of brightness dripping from his hair.

Rider.

Syocer trembled as she found the ground.

"Don't give up on me."

He surrendered his sword to the mottled earth as his hands cradled her head. There was nothing to say.

Airsing! *Evy…aelf …*

He quickly turned as two swords stared toward his heart; one belonged to him and a skeletal hand possessed the other.

The footsteps of his foe were the only thing prevalent in the silence of battle.

30

Sacrifice In A Word

Airsing rose.

The eyes lit in crimson as the swords pressed his ribs.

"Do you know how long I've waited to kill you? You-" his last words never found purpose as a blade ran through his chest; his eyes became an iridescent white as they seemed to lunge for him, smiling awkwardly.

The twisting hands shook as he leered, casting his hood down upon his disintegrating features; his soul fled into the darkness.

Arkt's tall frame was replaced by Zayin's intent sword that swallowed up the blood remaining on the blade.

"He's still alive." Zayin rekindled his energy as Airsing took his friend's arm, stabling his knees.

"Shoot ..."

Zayin's disappointment overshadowed his blade as he now wiped the blood from sight.

"I have to get her back."

Airsing's eyes were hollowing in white pupils, but were focused in single-mindedness as he looked through the deadening field onto Xavier's familiar silhouette.

"The war's almost over."

"Far from it," Airsing began.

"Airsing-"

Xavier ran upon the prospect, his quiver holding only one arrow as he inspected the ground for more ammunition.

"You still have the cloth?"

Xavier nodded.

"I'll show you."

Airsing now closed his eyes.

Syocer, keep holding on. Your will's strong.

Her eyes opened slightly as she looked into his own, which were smiling too sullenly.

My heart beats softly.

Her eyes closed as her head fell into his arms.

I'll take it.

Nyr. I won't let you. You won't sustain them.

Jx eklen.[25]

Airsing ...

He whispered a word, unfathomable, to her.

Wounds abruptly pierced his body as he felt the blades, though it was everything Syocer could do to keep him from them. His shirt instantly was engulfed in red as his skin was laid open from the cuts.

Lumos.

His eyes darkened as his last effort prevailed into the silence, *You would have died for me.*

"He's awake."

"How do you feel?"

"How would *you* feel?"

His focus came to, as his eyes secured on Syocer's wings over his hair.

"I feel like I fell five leagues off Syocer."

"Well, he still has his wits ..." Zayin remarked, "Drink this."

He took the soup-like concoction as he lifted it to his mouth; the broth was familiar.

"Have you all eaten?"

"We've been waiting for you."

"You all eat something. It's a strange sight to see food again ..."

---

[25] Literal meaning: My choice.

He smiled as he lifted his wrapped hands to Syocer's horse-like snout; his sore body became even more so as he was now aware of his surroundings.

31

The Long Awaited Blue Flame

"The cloth."

They were in a small cottage, having been given time to recuperate and eat. The fire was ablaze as he clutched the lightly knit material, gossamer in shape and purpose it seemed.

The cloth cracked as it had before, except the flame was blue and filled the room with a strange light.

"Whoa."

Xavier recoiled off his stance as a fireball soared just above his hair. He laughed with his one hand poised on the ground, his other upon his knee as he quickly evaded the fire devil.

Xavier peered across the room as he explained, "My…father told his superior that the spark had only one quality, which couldn't be unlocked but by the rider alone. This is why Arkt didn't kill you first ..."

He steadied his hand over a flame, soaking in the warmth as he continued, "…I know only one thing about his race: that when blood remains on the weapon, his defense mechanism kicked as he turned into the wind as a shadow. He's not of Syfrin blood; he's not even of this world. You'll have to use something other than what's known to this realm to conquer him.

"He's going to come back to kill you, even more thirsty and vengeful than before now that you've unlocked what he's been looking for. You and Syocer have to be ready. You're not only the last threat, but the last hope."

"I've heard that a lot ..."

They smiled as Zayin watched a spark that was eerily growing brighter.

Airsing held his hand over the blue flame that was soaring around the room; oddly enough, the fire halted under his hand.

He cupped the warmth in his wrapped palms as he carefully began to unravel them by rotating from bandage to finger to mouth. His hands were immaculate, except for a few scars remaining; the warmth carefully breathed light over his palms as he touched the fireball. The emanating object didn't burn him, but seemed to heal.

Syocer's eyes filled with white, as did Airsing's. He held onto the fire as streams of wind emanated from the spark.

The reflections of their eyes mirrored the spectacle perfectly; Syocer's wings covered Airsing's back as they were taken.

If the reader should want to take a small step into the darkness of what happens next, take the story's page by the edge and turn it. This next vision illuminates the future....

32

A Window To The Clash Of Worlds

Waking upon the darkness, he began to see a light flooding into his view. The luminescent glow drifted over the pictures his sight fell upon; he now noticed that the light was emanating from within him, like the day he perused the pages of that tunnel in Gnir.

But that was a long time ago ...

Or was it? He tried to sift through his memories, but all he could get out of his aching head was:

There was a blinding light...It filled my gaze until it felt like it was what I became.

He glanced at his fingertips as if noticing a spark about them.

It took me and- ...

His eyes now fluctuated, casting a ray of color through the light that projected from his sight.

Syocer?

Nothing echoed over his increasing uncertainty as Airsing struggled upward, persisting in his thought patterns.

Syocer, I can sense you...though you're not here ...

Airsing...Airsing ...

I can't reach you; you're too far away...What is this place?

Nothing responded.

Airsing now sensed a shadow enter the darkness; he cast his gaze around the room, but there was nothing there. He closed his eyes and reopened them as they emanated even more vividly, white as lightning to a stormy sky; dusk was no longer present in the extent.

Still nothing was there, or so it was to his Arqyn sight.

Sucöf.

Sucöf.

Syocer's two eyes oscillated in brightness as they were now imprinted in Airsing's mind, giving way to his new sense of sight: a brighter form of vision that could reflect over the unseen.

Airsing now noticed a dark creature leering at him in anger; this form was perplexedly aware that he had some tie to Airsing, wandering about the room as it tried to hide from the lightening glance of his watchful gaze.

"Airsing ..." the shadow now stepped into the intense pulses of light as it slyly continued: "What makes you different that you would fight for these so that the generations would live? You could become a greater emblem of hope if you would live under *me*."

Arkt's façade fell to the ground, as his old appearance no longer shuddered at the light glowing from Airsing's eyes.

You were much like your father...insolent. Give me your key and you can rule the world-as it was: you will not do so...You will die! Death is your only purpose in this life, Airsing...Let's hope it will be a quick one!

Airsing could read his mind, passive though he was; this supernatural ability did not occur by his own efforts.

Lumos, lyntry...kÿrni eks thyn ta![26]

"You ready, then?" Airsing's voice portrayed a distinct difference in his character, though his integrity and all still remained untainted.

"Boy, I'm always ready."

Arkt's skeletal hand reached for his crimson blade as he whipped it through the air, jocundly waving it in front of Airsing's face.

"The question, rather, should be: are you ready to die?"

---

[26] This phrase has stumped many for centuries, but has been thought of as: Warrior's Light, fight...to the end of all!

"Only too ..." Airsing rejoined, keeping his blade in its sheath long enough that Arkt wondered if this was going to be all too easy.

Then, Arkt took the first move as Airsing swiftly drew his sword into the phantom's blade, seeing the blood on the sharp edge come to life again.

"See it, boy! Relive it!"

Arkt's thirsty vengeance pinned the knife against him as Airsing struggled under the force, seeing the untold story replay in his head:

"Airsing!" Soren's voice rang clearly throughout the structure, leveling off as the silence quelled the once strong tone.

Airsing peered up toward his adversary; he was drinking in Airsing's thoughts with pleasure as they took him for another turn:

Now Soren's eyes were fixed upon the lifeless figure on the ground: his mother.

She was now unrecognizable as the woman he first saw in the dream:

Soren's pain reverberated from within him, starving him to the point of death.

Airsing looked away for a moment, not wanting to turn the light of his eyes upon the scene that lay fixed before him.

"Let it fill you ..." Arkt's voice was now drawing the very air into its submission.

Airsing's light slashed up again as he saw a poor reflection in Arkt's cracking eyes.

Without warning, Airsing broke into a fury that harnessed every inch of his strength, slashing the air with everything he had as Arkt faltered under his own parry.

Without a word, Airsing withdrew his blade as Arkt recoiled.

Airsing, breathing now choppy, looked upon the dark image as it stood up innocently. The figure smiled clandestinely as the picture before Airsing started to lunge for him.

Airsing rebuked him with a slash of his sword, waxing on the thought of killing this creature.

Arkt struck Airsing's high cheekbone with his blade as blood trickled down to his bitter taste. Airsing then straightened up as he held his sword over his shoulder, carrying a strengthening light that the figure before him knew not of; Airsing's blade now broke in two as it crushed through Arkt's heart.

Arkt stood resolutely smiling as if nothing had happened, holding the sword's very hilt in his hands; Arkt pulled the shards from his chest, whipping his black hair from his eyes. He laughed slightly as he didn't even wince, his shadow portraying strength into Airsing's jaded features.

"I'm of Shadowfax blood…and more; I don't die …" a trickle of crimson spilt from Arkt's mouth as he closed his vision away from the brightness, breathing in the deep air of the cave.

He now released his eyes, black as they were, acknowledging that the blood had disappeared.

"What now?"

Airsing's features looked up as he almost fell at the mercy of the lassitude that so gripped him. He blinked as he began to sense a familiar feel bringing life back into his thoughts.

Syocer's scales were so evident to his touch that he knew she had to be there with him, but nothing existed to spur this hope any further than it had already been encouraged.

Airsing looked up into Arkt's frozen features as he felt Syocer's mind probe into his.

Sucöf, mnya[27] *Lumos…Sucöf.*

Sucöf …

Airsing looked straight into Arkt's eyes as they faded into dust, his figure's disintegrating form bowing mockingly toward Airsing; Arkt's soul disappeared as it had done so long ago…or was it that long ago?

Airsing now fell to the ground, sword in pieces, as he cupped his face in his tired hands, working his fingers through his hair. His breathing steadied now as he focused on the floor, feeling a jarring tremor scorch his nerves.

A trickling noise fell upon Airsing's ears as he felt an overshadowing force envelope him.

---

[27] Literal meaning: my or great.

Printed in the United States
213287BV00001B/16/P

9 781606 935873